I0621485

TO

DANIEL MANUS PINKWATER

Ye Onlie Begetter

INGREDIENTS

First Words ——6

Threeword ——10

Proramble ——18

CHAPTERS

I: How Our Nameless Hero Left His Native Land ——19
II: The Housekhulaks… and Beyond ——21
III: A Dissertation Upon Roast Pie ——25
IV: A Suspect Passage ——28
V: Disaster! ——29
VI: Drifting and Mumbling ——30
VII: The Shore of _____ ——32
VIII: Flotsam Report ——35
IX: From Rags to Britches ——36
X: The Old, Odd Beachhouse ——38
XI: A Dumpstead Mystery ——39
XII: A Nameless Altar Ego ——40
XIII: The Great Riot of Pie Haven ——44
XIV: Travel Log ——45
XV: Flotsam Report # 2 ——46
XVI: The Shore of _____ (De nouveau) ——47
XVII: Concerning the Customs of the Skazeracs ——48
XVIII: Close Encounter of the Worst Kind ——51
XIX: Star Whirls ——52
XX: Star Whorls ——54
XXI: Star Wells ——55
XXII: The Coming of Batter Times ——57
XXIII: Chronologic Cookery ——59
XXIV: The Inedible Umbrella ——62
XXV: The Conga Line, or Lucky Lindsay ——64
XXVI: Meanwhile, Back at the Isle ——65

QUEST FOR THE PASTRIED PEACH

Rendered, in the manner of fat, from the oral tradition, being a fantasia upon the
Shaggy Jokester's Candide

y clept
SIBERIAN PEACH PIE

And, in its variant version,
BAVARIAN CREAM PIE

With divers shaggy concerns en route

Committed by
Marvin Kaye, OEKB*

who is y clept below as
Yr. Humble Piescribe

with Illustrations by
Marc Bilgrey

and a Threeword by
Jon Koons

*Old Enough to Know Better

This is an original publication of Metamorphic Press

Cover Art and Book Design by StrikingImages.com
Illustrations by Marc Bilgrey

ISBN: 978-1-951221-13-3

First Edition printing September, 2020

Published by:
Metamorphic Press
PO 151 Box
Tenafly, NJ 07670
metamorphicpress.com

Proudly Printed in the United States of America

XXVII: Lights Out! ——66
XXVIII: How to Secure an African Shrink ——68
XXIX: A Lad Who Used His Head ——70
XXX: From Sea to Shiny Sea ——72
XXXI: The Moscow Connection ——74
XXXII: So Close! ——80
XXXIII: Vathek the Hell? or, Dis Mus' Be de Blace! ——81
XXXIV: Caesarian Section ——83
XXXV: The Pasha's Peculiar Passion ——86
XXXVI: Bone Appetit ——90
XXXVII: Tale of the Poor Sharecropper ——98
XXXVIII: A Decidedly Shaggy Chapter ——104
XXXIX: The Shaggy Dog Lecture ——109
XL: The Exemplary Lecture of Abraham Grandbody ——112
XLI: A Nameless Reprise ——127
XLII: Theme, with Variations ——130
XLIII: The Final Speaker ——132
XLIV: Interramble – re Joyce! ——133
XLV: The Bavarian Cream Pie Story ——134
XLVI: The Bavarian Cream Pie Recipe ——135
XLVII: A Stony Ultimatum ——137
XLVIII: Much Adieu About Crusting ——138
XLVIX: The First Slice ——141
L: Is That a Faulkt? ——142
LI: A Farewell to Harms ——144
LII: Way Too Weird for a Title ——145
LIII: The Beginning of the End ——147
LIV: Countdown ——148
LV: The Quest Fulfilled? ——149
LVI: Why Is This Chapter Different
                from All Other Chapters? ——151
LVII: Finale Ultimo, i. e., Ye Punchline! ——152

Last Words ——153

Cryptic Advice on the Punchline ——161

FiRST WORDS

I first heard Siberian Peach Pie (one hesitates to call it a joke) in the 1950's, when I was either a student at Upper Darby Junior or Senior High School in suburban Philadelphia. I was surely a teenager, a fact to bear in mind when one considers the nature of the tale. The fellow who told it was a pal of one of my closest friends, the late, lamented David Goldenberg, model for Marty Gold, pharmacist detective of my two novels, My Son the Druggist and My Brother the Druggist. I only met Bruce Levitt on a few occasions, but am indebted to him for giving me (with a lot of noodjing from Dave) a copy of my all-time Number One book collector "want," Ray Bradbury's rare first short story collection, Dark Carnival, which Ray eventually personally inscribed to me, so at least I improved the "property."

One evening, possibly when we couldn't afford to go to the movies, at Dave's urging, Bruce told me the Siberian Peach Pie story. It took him over an hour to do so. It was and still is the most protracted shaggy dog tale I have ever heard or told.

Many years later, I came across a book that claimed the distinguishing characteristic of shaggy dog jokes is that they must possess an element of fantasy, but I think a better definition is what I found in Webster's Dictionary of the English Language Unabridged: "a humorous anecdote with a surprise ending involving ludicrously unreal or irrational behaviour." That is a fair description of the story Bruce told me, as well as other examples I have heard or devised. I would add that the most essential element of shaggy dog stories is that they must end with a ridiculous, anticlimactic punch-line, or in another joke Bruce told (which he called "the original shaggy dog story", which I am sure it is not), there was no punch-line at all. But I leave it to Mr. Abraham Grandbody to discuss the genre in greater detail in one of the latter installments of the story itself.

Quite a few years after I heard Siberian Peach Pie, my then literary agent, William B. Reiss, of the John Hawkins Agency, acquainted me with a variant he called Bavarian Cream Pie. Its plot-line differs considerably from the peachy version, but its punch-line is identical. Similarly, a website about shaggy humour traces a rather different plot-line for the peach pie tale.

Over the years, I have not only told Siberian Peach Pie many times, but have enormously expanded its Candide-ish plot with each retelling. The last time I told it was at a summer arts camp, and I managed to stretch it out into daily installments that lasted several weeks, on the theory that half the fun is not just getting there, but considering the tale's stunningly awful punch-line, getting there is perhaps the story's only virtue. As for that wretched punch-line, anyone who already knows it is requested to refrain from telling it to those who are as yet unfamiliar with the story; let them suffer the way we did. One word of warning – if you ever tell Siberian Peach Pie aloud, before you reveal the punch-line, be sure that you have planned a swift, safe exit route! Meanwhile, to ensure that readers of this tome will not peek at the punch-line prematurely, it has been written in code.

The verbal Siberian Peach Pie story that I've related over the years only serves as background for Quest for the Pastried Peach, which is much more protracted than any oral version I have ever told. Its origin traces back to a lengthy correspondence that took place in the 1980's between me and Daniel Pinkwater, this book's dedicatee, and a gentleman whom I consider to be one of America's greatest humorists. If you have not yet discovered his happily huge body of writing, hie thee to a Barnes & Noble or go on-line and treat yourself to Alan Mendelsohn the Boy from Mars, Blue Moose, Fat Men from Space, The Hoboken Chicken Emergency, Lizard Music, The Worms of Kukumlima, Young Adults, etc., etc., etc.

At some point in our voluminous body of bouffes lettres, I discovered that Mr. Pinkwater was not familiar with Siberian Peach Pie, and he urged me to relate it to him, which I proceeded to do over the course of many months. The result, with more than a little in the way of later emendation from an older, perhaps more experienced, but certainly wearier yours truly, is the Quest for the Pastried Peach. Its excesses include literary buffoonery (see Last Words) ranging from inept to hyperbolic, an humongous foot-note based on Bruce Levitt's "original shaggy dog story," a digression that includes my own "take" on Bavarian Cream Pie, and a great number of insufferable anecdotes ending in puns that mostly I devised with another old friend, Toby Sanders, author of Stein & Day's How to Be a Compleat Clown, though one section was published in the 1983 program book of Balticon 17, a Baltimore-based science-fantasy convention. (Again, see Last Words.)

Another friend, Jon Koons, a multi-talented writer, magician, puppeteer, et cetera, was one of the summer arts attendees who heard the story the last time I told it. At his urging, and with considerable difficulty (the manuscript only exists as faint onionskin copies of the original letters I sent to Dan Pinkwater), I have prepared the Quest for the Pastried Peach. So, hey, blame him, not me. Jon suggested he contribute a Foreword, but that struck me as too formal and legitimate for the ensuing monsterpiece, so, cranking back on his suggestion, Jon contributed a Threeword, instead. (His Dad, the estimable Irv Koons, suggested he make it a Three + word, but Jon demurred, though I hope he did not accuse his father of putting in his two cents, for a plus sign, I should think, is only the equivalent of a ha'penny.)

—Marvin Kaye - New York City, 2009-11

THREEWORD

Concerning the Matter of Yr. Humble Piescribe
and his Peachy Pilgrimage

As I am, in the First Words above, given blame for the goading of the Piescribe into finally putting pen to paper (so to speak) and once and for all piescribing the tome into which you are about to plunge, I felt it appropriate to explain and potentially defend myself.

I met Marvin Kaye when I was an impressionable young teen at the performing arts camp mentioned above, back in the days when people were still wearing leisure suits. It is an experience from which I have never fully recovered. As commander of a troupe of Magic Program geeks, Marvin, noted magician and author of magic books that he was, held the awesome responsibility of shaping this rag-tag band of teens into Magicians Par Excellence, ready to entertain and amaze generations to come. That I am still out there doing magic and making much of my living at it would suggest he was at least partially successful. Still, this was an unenviable position to be in, fraught with perpetual mischiefs committed, foul deeds perpetrated, and riotous mayhem ensuing. We students caused some of it as well. Not simply content to hone our magical and performance skills, Marvin took it upon himself to sculpt our malleable young minds and souls. To hammer, twist and warp them into some shape that might be just odd and eccentric enough to make it in "The Biz", or indeed, in life. It is here where the fabled pie of peach first entered into my consciousness.

A couple of weeks into the summer, already weary of cut and restored ropes, French Drops, spring flowers, flash paper and fanning powder (if you know not to what I refer, track down a copy of the *Stein & Day Handbook of Magic* and have at it), our fearless (or was it feckless?) leader, aided and abetted by the above referenced Toby Sanders, our clown and circus guru, embarked upon an ambitious agenda meant to broaden us, presenting for us the most unusual, and often inappropriate (might have said the parents) literature imaginable. During brief daily intermissions from our theatrical training and rehearsals, in which other campers were swimming or participating in sports or just generally doing camp-like things, the magic/circus gang were gathered together in one of several varied venues for a daily fix. Toby would read us installments of Robert Shiarella's *Your Sparkle Cavalcade Of Death*, a wonderfully warped and satirical novel of questionable morality, and Marvin, in the age-old storyteller tradition, would confer upon us and extemporize on the tale of the Siberian Peach Pie.

Marvin's daily installments became the highlight of our days, being dragged along with his Nameless Hero through the snows of Siberia, the frigid waters of sundry oceans, and to colorful (psychedelic even) locations real and imagined around the cosmos. With improbable situations and tortuous tangents becoming more and more absurd along the way, we lapped it up. (It was more fun, at any rate, than archery or basket-weaving.) On rare, precious occasions we might even get two segments in a single day! Marvin managed to weave his tale and stretch it out for weeks, with foreseeably endless installments ranging in length from scant minutes to seemingly hours. How he accomplished this and actually captured and held the attention of this largely Bar Mitzvah age cluster of ragamuffins, is still beyond my ken. And so the summer went, with Marvin's declamations, characterizations, gesticulations and assorted other -ations filling my mind with thoughts and imaginings unlike any I had theretofore thought or imagined.

On one of the last days of camp, possibly the penultimate, as campers were grudgingly readying themselves for the unwelcome trip back to parents, school and the drudgery of reality in general, and councillors, so long deprived of life's worthier pursuits of sex, drugs, rock 'n' roll, and the like, were eagerly anticipating return to their own realities, the magic and circus misfits gathered for the last time to hear the much anticipated and conjectured upon final chapter of Siberian Peach Pie. After six or more weeks of the perilous adventures of our Nameless Hero– who had by now become our friend, our docent, and the very fulcrum in the seesaw of life, instilling in us desire and the knowledge that any goal worth attaining is attainable, no matter how unlucky or inept the seeker might be– we knew that there was going to be a triumphant finale and one hell of an incredible punch line. As we sat, one and all, gathered for the last time thus, outside on the second story deck, with Marvin standing before us, hyperbolizing and embellishing for the last time, winding to a close a journey that we had begun eons before, the scene took on an almost surrealistic guise. As his voice boomed and his gestures became ever more expansive, bright sunlight from behind surrounded our frenetic fabulist with an unearthly aura, into which he seemed almost to recede. The tension in the air was palpable. The moment of ultimate punchline was upon us. Time for the zinger! Marvin seemed even more receded than formerly. It took me a moment to realize that this was no trick of the light, but that Marvin was actually backing, very slowly and deliberately, towards the far end of the deck and the steps. At the final moment of revelation, when the punchline had been delivered– there was a moment of strained silence. Then the mild mannered group turned suddenly ugly, and as if instantly and simultaneously lycanthropized, rose as one. I have rarely seen anyone before or since move as fast as Marvin did. He was down the steps and out of sight before we reached the landing.

It is several years later. I have always remembered, and had tried, somewhat unsuccessfully, to retell the Siberian Peach Pie tale a few times over the years. My endurance and impromptu imaginings never seemed up to the task. Plus, vital details of Marvin's memorable tale had succumbed to the ravages of time and the shriveling of little grey cells, and were, sadly, no longer rememberable. And then Marvin and I perchance became reacquainted. The precise details of this rediscovery have now escaped me. It is an experience from which I have never fully recovered. After a "cold reading" audition he had requested of me, Marvin was duly impressed with my dramaturgy and command of language (even though I had pronounced "gunwales" as spelled), and I was granted the honor of becoming a member of The Open Book, NYC's first Performing-With-Script-In-Hand-To-Link-Literature-And-Drama Theatre Company. I had the inestimable pleasure of acting with Marvin, under his direction, and in plays scripted by his own hand. Also stage managing, doing props, costumes, box office, making coffee... So, once again I was Marvin's willing minion. His Renfield. Or as colorful contemporary street parlance might have it, His Bitch. My renewed association with Count Emkay the Miraculous (for he was, and is, none other) re-kindled my desire for Peach Pie. But Marvin was reticent, and never did reembark upon the Pie trail.

I became a fan of Marvin's writing, and attended his scholarly classes in the art of the assembly of words. We collaborated on TV pitches. He became my literary mentor, and indeed commissioned my story "The Adventure Of The Missing Countess", for his anthology *The Game Is Afoot:*

Pastiches, Parodies and Ponderings of Sherlock Holmes. I considered Marvin a true and respected friend. But why wouldn't he tell me the tale of the Nameless Hero, dammit? Perhaps he just couldn't find the six weeks in his schedule in which to tell it, or thought not to be able to do it justice in an abbreviated form. He should just write it all down for Pete's sake...! Eureka! My campaign began. I petitioned relentlessly for the tale to be told in print, but to no avail. At one point I finally lost hope that Marvin might ever relent, so I called him for a few, please, please, brief reminders of the story of the Pie, because I would write it myself.

I decided to write the story for children, having been successful previously with my children's books, and therefore assuming I would have an "in" with the publisher. My initial attempt to bake my pie resulted in an insipid pastry, bland and tasteless. The crusting was limp and flaccid. The less than delectable filling was runny and pedestrian. It was, in truth, half baked. (I could go on, but I think I've beaten this metaphor near to death.) It began with an elementary explanation of the form, thus:

> I want to tell you a joke. It's not like any joke you've ever heard. You see, it's called a "shaggy dog story", and when you do it right it takes ages to tell. My friend Marvin told it to me. He told me a little bit at a time, and it took him a couple of months. When he finally did get to the punchline I was so mad I chased him all the way home. Then, after that, we laughed and laughed and laughed. You see, the point of a shaggy dog story is to stretch it out, make stuff up, let it get crazier and crazier, and then finally, after a long time, end with a punchline that is a real "groaner"— one that makes everyone groan because it's so bad. But the punchline isn't the

point... it's getting there that's all the fun. If you can read only one section of this book every day you'll understand! So I'm going to tell my own version of the story, but when you tell it to others you should be creative and make up stuff and make the joke your own. And remember, only tell a little bit at a time, make it last— and plan your escape route— so that when you finally do get to the punchline, after all that build up, your friends will chase you all the way home!

After writing a chapter or two, try as I might, most of what I came up with seemed to pale by comparison with my remembrances of the tale as told by the Master. And as a kid's book, for this current device-carrying, Tik-Tok, Instawhatever obsessed generation, it required so much explanation as to things like what a door-to-door salesman was, why he might need to stick his foot in the door, and why anyone would buy a vacuum cleaner from him, that in it's infancy I was already losing steam. How much would I have to explain to make this work? Although I was pleased with much of what I had penned, especially the naming of his product— the Electro-Modern Happy Suck Super Deluxe Vacuum Cleaner— life and circumstances (just little things, like adopting a son...) bade me put the project on the back burner. And there it sat for a couple of years, until I unexpectedly got an e-mail from Marvin, at once exultant and accusatory, announcing that he had finally done it. He had given new life to the story to which I had aspired.

"Dear Jon... you actually suggested that I do what I just finished a few minutes ago... I will admit it was more fun than I expected, and I want you to be the very first to see it... And if you don't like it, remember, it's really your fault!"

And like lightning striking neck bolts, *Quest for the Pastried Peach* was born. Now, finally, others would know my pain. With a light heart I took my own version off the burner and placed it into the deep freeze in anticipation of the long awaited yarn as could only be spooled out by, to my mind, it's originator. I read it. It is an experience from which I have not yet fully recovered.

As I began to read, intoxicants at the ready in case of emergency, I was swept away in a whirlwind of ingenious nonsensica. Using an inspired montage of literary styles, homages, and esoteric references, Marvin had ingeniously minced together anecdotes, jokes, puns and uncanny states of affair into a frothy shaggy dog stew that brought back memories which made me long for senility. I read the text on my laptop, and was therefore prevented by my common sense (read: wife) from flinging the thing across the room, as I had desperately desired to do on no less than three occasions. (This I have done before whilst perusing various of Marvin's other books, and is, I understand, a common occurrence for readers of some of his more puntacular entries.) Using situations and turns of phrase that would do Douglas Adams or P.G.Wodehouse proud, and including an interminable tangential footnote the likes of which even Terry Pratchett might envy, I think *Quest for the Pastried Peach* should be counted among the most entertaining, creative, humorous, perspicacious, pointless and silliest books ever perpetrated upon the general populous since the dawn of time. But then again I would have to say that regardless, as I am given full marks as its instigator.

I was honored when Marvin asked me (by way of me begging him) to write the Threeword for this book. Initially, when he was dubious about me writing a Foreword, my name perhaps not being a household enough one to warrant the full prestige and awesome responsibility, I suggested that, in this day and age of rampant downsizing, a Threeword might suffice. He agreed with a hearty guffaw, and exhorted me to write my Threeword, although in retrospect I can't be certain he didn't actually say "write three words." So why did I tenaciously volunteer to write this? Is it because Marvin is a considerably above average writer versed in so many genres who I admire greatly? No. Is it because I consider Marvin my "Literary Mentor" who has inspired and instructed me, and first published me? Nah. Is it because Marvin is and has been one of my dearest, most valued friends for so many years? Nope. Is it because Marvin helped shape me into the person I am today? Certainly not! (I shudder at the thought.) I have expended my time and creative juices to laud Marvin and his latest masterpiece for the purest of reasons. I hope to impress his agent so that she'll take me on and get more of my own books published. Oh, and because I really liked the book. I'm sure that you, gentle reader, as you consume the delightful confection that is *Quest for the Pastried Peach* (intoxicants at the ready in case of emergency) will also really like the book, and be warped, twisted and swept away as I was. It will be an experience from which you will likely never fully recover.

Once more, dear friends, unto the peach.

—Jon Koons - November 2010

PRORAMBLE

A destiny that leads from 'Frisco-town
About the pendant world, both up and down,
From foulest strand anon to fairest shore—
A quest is tried, unequaled nevermore!
I sing of arms, and truth to tell, of legs,
Of cannibals and kings, of life, its dregs;
I'll sing this day till time and tide are done,
From gleaming morning knife to *SUNSET GUN*.[1]
A goodly youth, well seasoned in his art,
Forth from his native land shall soon depart;
He wotteth not his journey will be long
(As thou must wot; if not, rescan this song.)
We go now, you and I, to 'Frisco beach,
Where this begins, the Quest for Pastried Peach.

---

[1] Capitalized and italicized because it is the title of one of Dorothy Parker's books of mostly humorous poems. Which has nothing whatsoever to do with this book.

HOW OUR NAMELESS HERO LEFT HIS NATIVE LAND

I n old San Francisco, there dwelt a young gentleman whom Nature endowed with the most gentle character and a face whose expression reflected his simple soul.

He desired nothing more than to eke from the pocketbooks of his fellow men a modest living that might support him in rudimentary fashion and the provender to which he was accustomed: Burgers a la King, Chicken a la Colonel, Tacos a la Bell, and similar modest fare.

Of course he could not stint those necessaries of civilization expected of the good citizenry of the California territory; to keep abreast of his neighbors he must needs maintain a basic household of 1 wife, 2 children, 2.5 mistresses, a 1.3 year old auto, 1 Harmon-Kardon turntable with Pickering cartridge[2], 1 above-ground Coleco swimming pool (to be built; space reserved in his back yard), 2 picnic tables, 1 doghouse habited by an 8-foot stuffed canine, and 1 tap for piped-in beer.

It occurred to our Nameless hero— to be precise, Algernon Q. (for Quincy) Nameless— that it was meet he should seek gainful employment to attain and maintain said necessaries. He sought throughout the valley, but in the land there had come to pass a Grand Recession, complete with quadrilles and lancers, and he was sore put to findeth a job.

In desperation, he petitioned a fashioner of vacuum cleaners to make use of his hypothetical abilities. It was a fateful moment in his life. In the corrupted currents of this world, where most things go awry, a cosmic cam indeed slipped, and he was hired to sell his principal's product.

Now salesmanship is a common American occupation that everyone instinctively distrusts. But this at least was not a trial our Nameless hero had to face. Instead, he was told to develop for his firm a new market, one whose natives were untrained in the above-said distrusts.

And thus, A. Q. Nameless was sent by banana boat (a wholly inappropriate craft, by the way) to unload his quantity of electric dust-suckers in the vasty frozen reaches of Siberia.

---

[2] This is obviously a period piece, though chronologically inaccurate.

THE HOUSEKHULAKS...
AND BEYOND

They call it Piskwasser. The natives are known familiarly as Piskallehs, or Lilipisks, or just Piskers. I call it cold as a landlady's attic flat. It's Siberia, and I don't like it.

I'm Nameless. I sell Little Wonder Spotless Carpet Machines. Vacuum cleaners.

I hit town at 8:30 am local time. By 8:07, the town hit me. Specifically, several doors whomped my ankles.

knock

The door creaked wide. A gnarled, wizened, crooked, knock-kneed, splay-footed, bandylegged, round-shouldered, humpbacked, snub-nosed, stumpy, bloated, and altogether disproportionate old crone eyed me balefully.

She was indescribable.

"Yah, sonneyevitch, votcha vant?"

I threw my sales-pitch.

She caught it with her door-slam.

She won the inning.

All the Housekhulaks were the same. I didn't sell them bupkis.

But that afternoon, a spectacular change of fortune! A cherubic bucolic decided the Little Wonder Spotless Carpet Machines could profitably be adapted and sold as containers for dispensing or dispersing manure, depending on whim, need, or predilection. He bought the entire lot![3]

Ye Transitional Passage;
Returning unto 3rd Person

Now when our hero divested himself of his stock, it occurred to him that he would be full sore delighted to getteth the hell home, so he betook himself unto the closest railroad station that could connect him with Vladivostok, where he proposed to embark on the first available ship.

Unfortunately, that year the trains were only running in July, so he had a bit of a wait as it was June 30th. He decided to explore the town.

The reader must bear in mind that these adventures took place many long years ago ... this being by way of explanation of the ensuing sight that A. Q. Nameless witnessed as he journeyed through the town.

Ye Sight:

Fifty mighty Cossacks storming along on their hoarses (sic)[4], spitting upon the peasants, and shouting, "Hail the Czar! Down with the Bolsheviks!" As Nameless gave them wide

---

[3] This first-person account by A. Q. Nameless as discovered in the ruins of his beach house (q. v., below) sheds new and important light on his history. Formerly, all raconteurs of the Siberian Peach Pie root-story assumed he sold his vacuum cleaners without difficulty to the Housekhulaks. But this always seemed suspicious to me, due to the dearth of electricity in Siberia.

[4] Mathologic animals you can't count on. (Daniel Pinkwater, original recipient of this story claimed he owned said beasts, hence this sarcaustic referent.)

berth and returned to the town's small business district, he espied a large sign.

Ye Sign:

SIBERIA RESTAURANT
Cooler Inside!

It is conjectured that our hero had a Nameless hunger. Let metaphysicians debate the point. At any rate, he opened the restaurant's door and entered.

A DISSERTATION UPON ROAST PIE

Mankind, saith a rare manuscript which my friend DMP was obliging enough to read and comment thereupon, for the first seventy thousand years or more of prehistory, ate pie baked, just as they mostly do in America to this day.

But the manuscript claims that there once was a peddler whose name is lost to history who betook himself to an eatery y clept Siberia Restaurant (Cooler Inside) and whiled away the time till his train arrived by feasting on various local comestibles, which mainly consisted of soup made from beets and beer.

At the end of said meal, the Nameless peddler inquired whether for dessert they might have some kind of succulent pastry, and the host laughed, for it was evident his guest was a stranger to the area and therefore did not know that the town was famous for its local bakery, TastTKossak, which prided itself on its Siberian Peach Pie, made at considerable expense from imported Siberian peaches and yak milk. It was customary to serve it warm, so the host placed a generous portion in the oven, where a roast beet (sic) (indeed) roast was turning on the spit.

At length, the smoldering dessert was served to the peddler, who both eyed and sniffed it suspiciously. The aroma was unique!

He felt the pie gingerly to see whether it was too hot to eat yet. It was … he burned his fingers, and thrust them into

his mouth to cool them. And thus, for the first time, did the Nameless peddler taste roast Siberian Peach Pie.

It was delicious beyond comprehension, a pie that passeth understanding: ecstasy and nirvana rollèd into crusting like a shantih-chant! The peddler surrendered himself to pleasure, and fell to tearing off great gobbets of outer flake and inner sweet. With every bite, he took in air and swirled about his cheeks like a wine taster releasing the full bouquet of digestible perfection.

Upon finishing the last crumb, dollop and shard, he knew he had reached a crossroad in his life, for he was totally hooked on Siberian Peach Pie. He could not conceive another meal without it. He stared morosely at his empty plate, which he had indeed licked clean.

The peddler asked the host for a second piece, but that worthy explained that the one he'd eaten was the last in the restaurant. The bakery was many miles away over wintry fields and woodland, and its next shipment was not due till the following week.

The Nameless peddler disconsolately quit the premises.

It hath long been argued, states the rare manuscript, that the proper way to eat roast Siberian Peach Pie is with a fork, but many believe that the Nameless peddler adopted the original and proper tradition of hoisting that basic implement known to mankind— a finger.

IV

A SUSPECT PASSAGE

An oral tradition claims that Nameless's visit to the Siberian Restaurant (Cooler Inside) was distinguished by this exchange:

"What y' want for dessert?"

"What y'got?"

"Siberian Peach Pie."

"What else?"

"Nothing else."

"Hot town. What do you all do for excitement? Come here and eat the pie?"

"That's right."

"Smart boy. You think you're smart?"

"Yeah, pretty smart."

"Well, I think you're dumb."

"If you say so."

"I say so."

"Okay, I'm dumb."

"Good. Now get the pie."[5]

---

[5] Editor's Note: This dialogue is suspect because it has not been proven that Nameless could speak Siberian, or any variety of Russian. Further, it is unlikely that the restaurateur spoke English, which was then illegal in Siberia. Also it is highly improbable he would have been familiar with the expression, "Okay," which was coined circa 1840 in re: (Old) Kinderhook, New York, birthplace of Martin Van Buren. If you don't believe Yr. Humble Piemage, look it up.

V

DISASTER!

From a taped transcription of "Dateline: Disaster!," a syndicated radio show by W. Windchill Factor, columnist, commentator and harbinger of doom.

" ...ship filled with people just like you and me, Mr. and Mrs. Average American. Hoping the dreams they all hope. Dreading the fears they all dread. Thinking the thoughts they all think. Like you and like me. Men like Harry B. Peckersniff, tycoon and popcorn baron. Down to the deeps he went, his empire too small, as the Bard might put it. Too small to save him from Davy Jones's locker. Men like A. Q. Nameless, vacuum cleaner salesman. Flushed with the success of a brilliant first foray into new territory. Determined to get new product from his West Coast employer, turn around and go right back to Siberia. Sole survivor Captain Mantelpiece particularly remembered Nameless. Said the Cap: "That guy was always at the rail, shoving at it, as if to make the ship go faster. Mumbling something under his breath." Yes, Mr. and Mrs. America, those muttered words... a secret we will never know, lost on that fatal voyage when the iceberg tore a hole in the side of the ship... "

Vi

DRiFTiNG AND MUMBLiNG

Only those who spend their lives at sea can fully appreciate the cruelties of Dame Ocean, that grand harbinger of mysteries collectively known as the Pacific.

Driftwood. Imagine clusters of ash scattered about a large parking lot. Call the parking lot the ocean and those ashes all that is left of a great ship. In the midst of the churning turmoil, one sentient thing splashes and twists, tiny beneath the cerulean blanket that covers the sea with a skyful of sky. Amassed cumulus looks down, bemused, at shards of intentions, blasted, wrecked.

The Nameless sentience clings to broken timber also adrift in the drink. Half-conscious, rocked and rolled by breaking swells and swelling breakers toward some destination only known to the Spirit of the Deep. But what it knows, it says not. It just lies low.

From the drifter's lips ariseth a bubble of sound, and then another– syllables drawn from someplace deep within. Random sound lost in the endless canvas of saltspume and crying gulls. A single word repeated over and over again, a lost litany to the lane-end of Nameless dreams…

" … pie… pie… pie… "[6]

---

[6] Oral tradition does not render the two preceding chapters with such style, grace or verbosity. Here is the bald folk version: "So he went back to get more vacuum cleaners, hoping when he returned, the restaurant would have more pie. But his ship hit an iceberg, and the sea cast him onto The Shore of ____ ."

VII

THE SHORE OF ____

A bunch of the boys were whooping it up down by the Skazerac ice-floe…"

The fate of our Nameless flotsam upon The Shore of ____ [7] has been preserved in the above serviceable verse, but the facts are grimmer than its rhythmic swing would have us believe. The tale has been likened by some scholars to the problematic transmutation of the death of Balder into the gruesome children's rhyme, "Who Killed Cock Robin?"

For "a bunch of the boys," one must substitute a tribe of high-spirited, low-minded Skazeracs, who are related to the Eskimos, though the latter refuse to admit it. The "Skazerac ice-floe" refers (wholly inaccurately, as is often the case for poetry) to the isle itself (____), which is covered with ice most of the year. And what the poet calls "whooping it up" is a Bowdlerization of a bloody tribal ceremony.

The simple prose of the matter is this: the Skazeracs inhabit The Shore of ____ , which is a drifting Pacific island that in its eastern orbit has left skidmarks on the Ponapes before rerouting westward.

According to the tribe's oral tradition spat down from father to son (they once saw how kava was made and got the

---

[7] Like the French guttural "r" or African click-sounds, it is impossible to spell the name of the island, since the western palate cannot reproduce the Skazerac tongue, at least not when sober.

process all screwed up), a Nameless castaway was washed up onto their frozen shore. One of the tribe spoke English (a long story— don't ask!) and on the newcomer's awakening, he questioned him, but the only thing learned was that the stranger would be pleased to sell them all vacuum cleaners.

The tribal elders held council, and agreed that since food was scarce, their best course was to convert the Nameless one into that commodity. As they debated, their captive broke free because, according to the Skazerac idiom, he wished to "salvage his donkey."[8]

The hapless happener did manage to flee and ultimately quit the isle, though not before one particularly swift Skazerac runner drew close enough to hack off his left arm (i.e., "whooping it up") with his machete.[9]

Immediately thereafter, the injured adventurer splashed back into the Pacific.

---

[8] Truly an odd figure of speech, inasmuch as there are no donkeys on The Isle of ___ . One school of thought traces the expression to the English-speaking tribe member, but another Skazerac faction supports a metaphysical theory that raises even knottier questions since no form of Christianity exists in their culture, so how could they know anything about the Biblical legend of Balaam? In order to avoid halting our story's onrush, we shall quit this point for now, and return to it later.

[9] Made from the Skazerac's wood-pulp substance known as pippier. Thus their weapons are referred to as pippier-machetes.

Viii

FLOTSAM REPORT

TO: Herr Burgomeister, Town Hall

FROM: Abe Grandbody, resident lifeguard, beachmaster, physician and ice-cream salesman, Pismo Beach, CA[10]

IN RE: Flotsam

REPORT: At 6:30 a.m., during the morning tidewash, a Nameless body was cast up on P. B. I kicked it to test how far advanced it had decayed. To my surprise, it moaned. I examined the man (clothes were in tatters, so gender was easily determinable.) He is a young wild-eyed emaciated Caucasian lacking a left arm. Evidence of frostbite at the stump suggests it was cauterized in icy waters, possibly the Skazerac current, which is running more than usually off-course this year. Aspect of flotsam truly frightening: wild eyes, feral craftiness, incoherent mumbling of repeated one-syllable word.

DISPOSITION: Netted flotsam, remanded for corrective psychotherapy at Pismo Home for the Retarded.[11] Flotsam, being destitute, could not be admitted to county hospital, as he lacked any form of health insurance.

---

[10] "Pismo Beach ... a sand trap with a ferris wheel." – Bob Hope

[11] In the oral tradition, it is a home for aged hamsters, which, of course, is totally implausible.

iX

FROM RAGS TO BRiTCHES

From the weekly column by W. Windchill Factor in the Friscotown Post.

Surely no more inspiring story exists of the pure spunk and resourcefulness of our native youth than the re-rise and triumph of Algernon Q. Nameless, who went down in the U. S. S. Mantelpiece disaster, though he did not go down, but was reported drifting northward when last seen... until a lifeguard found him cast up on Pismo Beach.

One-armed.

Mindless.

Pantsless.

Two years of shock therapy restituted mind and memory, and Nameless hitched his way back to San Fran. Unfortunately, his lack of arm and pants made it impossible for him to regain his old job selling vacuum cleaners.

How, then, has he become one of the most respected tycoons in our community? What drove him to succeed as a beer-barrel baron?

Here are his own words.

"I didn't have a dime, or even an arm to beg for one," he confided. "But in my mind, W. W., I had one and only one thought! No less than a religious pilgrimage to Siberia!"

Like most visionaries, he began small. He was walking along the same beach where the ocean currents cast him up, when he saw the beginnings of his fortune in the sand.

A silver toothpick.

Soon after, Nameless encountered a beachcomber just completing the Sunday Acrostic. He offered his toothpick for his comb, but finally agreed to trade for the fellow's fountain pen.

Next, he met a woman whose pen was out of ink, and she wanted to complete the Sunday Crossword, so she traded Nameless a brass ruler for his pen.

By a process too tedious to outline in detail, Nameless kept trading up: the ruler for a yardstick, the yardstick for a fence-picket, and in this wise within three weeks he was the new owner of the Frisco Suburban Lumber Company, makers of 65% of all beer-barrels used west of the Rockies.

X

THE OLD, ODD BEACHHOUSE

Like glowing Noma Lites in a dead man's eyes, the baleful windows of Pie Haven shed saffron sickly illumination over the tumid headwaters of the Turgid River, this side of the beach where flows the mighty effluent of Nameless Suburban Lumber Company into the ocean (the Pacific, to be specific).

The old beachhouse, purchased not long before by the strange young owner of the lumber firm, sits waiting for its fell destiny to be fulfilled. Curses seep from every timber.

The Nameless wood-baron, a handicapped curmudgeon with one arm, retired to this beachhouse and shunned company, never inviting anyone to his retreat. Rumor has it that he built his empire on this unlucky site because a real estate agent told him that Pie Haven is the point in the United States furthest west and therefore closest to the Russian mainland.

His seclusion was disturbed by only one bit of public business: adverts in every periodical east and west:

SIBERIAN CHEF WANTED
Must be expert dessertologist

No one applied for the position.

XI

A DUMPSTEAD MYSTERY

C ut from the Greater Pie Haven Daily Telegraph

The neighborhood of Dumpstead... (which is five miles southeast of Bumpstead and a mere tern's throw from Pie Haven— ed.) is at present attempting to cope with a series of events just bordering on the annoying.

Some of its pre-teen population has been reported missing. The police state that in the past three weeks, sixteen young have disappeared, half of them from the Wallis T. McCutcheon clan. McCutcheon, 86, tersely commented, "Good riddance."

Alderman-elect Abernathy Rumbunny has sworn that if the disappearances do not stop, he will force his defeated opponent Abe Grandbody to take action. Grandbody has recently accepted the post of police chief for Pie Haven, county seat of Dumpstead.

Xii

A NAMELESS ALTAR EGO

I , Abe Grandbody, of sound body and mind, and fully possessed of my wits, grits, and teeth, solemnly attest to the events of the night of January 16th, recorded below.

1. Not Every Bagman is Santa Claus

Hizzoner assigned me to look into the case of the missing offspring of W. T. McCutcheon. I rounded up a triangle of square citizens, met them by my barbecue pit and organized a steakout.

Three nights passed without incident, but on the fourth night, just as the moon dipped behind steel-wool clouds overhanging Dumpstead, one of my crew, Fenris T. McCutcheon, 33rd cousin of W. T., screamed aloud near my waiting-post. Me and other guards, now fully awake, headed in the direction of the yell and spied a small, odd figure with a large burlap sack slung over his shoulder crossing the porch of W. T.'s house. As we drew closer, we could see we were dealing with a one-armed man. The bag he clutched was wriggling and emitted distressed muffled noises.

It looked suspicious. And where was Fenris?

2. Over Hill, Over Dale

We sidled and slunk after the nameless figure. The furtive fugitive led us a damp chase through dewy nightgrass, in and out of dunes, around cesspools, stopping only once at a hamburger stand, where he reemerged with a sack of food that he dumped into the burlap sack, out of which began to emerge crunching noises.

Curiouser and curiouser. Fenris loved burgers.

"Know what?" I said to my deputy, Lavinia Dappledipple. "I think he's got an animal in that sack."

Lavinia nodded, but then she often nodded off.

Our path led us directly to Pie Haven. In the distance loomed the odd, old beach house of that strange chap I'd rescued many years back from the sea.

I suddenly recalled that our quarry must be the very same fellow, for I remembered that the man I'd rescued (can't remember his name) was missing an arm.

At last, my team came to a halt as the lurching figure climbed the steep steps of his house at Pie Haven. He did not enter, but lugged his sack around the side of the building. We followed. Our pursuit took us to his back yard.

The moon emerged from the clouds and we saw the Nameless fellow standing by a huge platform and tying a young man to it.

"I'll be dogged," Lavinia whispered. "It's Fenris."

Now where the hell did he come from?

3. Bon Appetit

As Fenris stuffed his mouth with french fries, the little man flicked a switch and with a groan of metal and the chug of an engine, the platform Fenris lay tied to began to rise into the air. Looking up, I saw at the very top of the structure a mammoth statue of a slice of pie. Suddenly the platform shuddered and went into a near-perpendicular slant. Fenris slid down and disappeared into the pie, fries and all.

"O Mighty Great Siberian Peach Pie!" the little man prayed in a high, reedy voice, "Accept my sacrifice!"

The pie statue emitted a deafening sound which appeared to gratify its bizarre worshipper.

Crooning happily, he proclaimed, "Bon appetit!"

4. I Only Did My Duty

Lavinia and I and the rest of my team agreed that the religious rite we had just witnessed was probably connected with the so-called Dumpstead Mystery, so I reported the incident immediately to my brother, Milgrim, who published the Greater Pie Haven Daily Telegraph. He ran the story on page one.

I regret to report that this was the direct cause of the incident known as the Great Riot of Pie Haven. But I do not feel at all responsible.

After all, I was only doing my duty.

Xiii

THE GREAT RIOT OF PIE HAVEN
(more or less to the tune of "Finnegan's Wake")

There once was a man who had no name
He did some things all rather odd—
He fed some kids to his Pie-God,
And that is when his neighbors came.

They trussed him up, and what is more
They broke his statue. It was vile!
And as they did, they did not smile
For he had made them all quite sore!

CHORUS
O, whackerah! Blood and pie!
A brannigan y'never seen!
Isn't it the truth, I'm telling you?
They vented their collective spleen!

And as he quailed with great dismay
They took him to his lumber yard
They made it burn till it was charred
And beat him black and blue and grey

They tied him to a wooden board
And as their prey began to scream
They tossed him in a mighty stream
And off he floated to the fjord.
CHORUS

XIV

TRAVEL LOG

As the sun sets at Pie Haven Cove, a quantity of logs slides down a sluice in the middle of which is positioned a huge buzzsaw. One of the largest logs is curiously entwined with crisscrossed cords that appear to fasten a Nameless figure to the timber.

XV

FLOTSAM REPORT # 2

I tem: Found ashore at Pismo Beach – one oddly shaped bit of driftwood shaped like a leg, its stump so realistically hewn by the elements that its upper end looks exactly the way it might if it had been cauterized by the ocean's icy currents.

—submitted by A. Grandbody, D.O. (Demoted Official)

XVI

THE SHORE OF _____
(De nouveau)

Far from the shipping lanes and somewhere more or less in the middle of the Pacific one might or might not find The Isle of _____.

One twilight, there washed ashore a Nameless thing missing two limbs.

XVii

CONCERNING THE CUSTOMS OF THE SKAZERAC

Theologists, anthropologists and archeologists have long haggled over the significance of the so-called Wanderer God on The Isle of _____, but the thoughtful scholar surely must support the only viable theory: that it is a classic example of Deophagia.

The legend is as follows: once a Nameless castaway was washed up onto the beach of the island home of the Skazeracs. It was a season of great deprivation when game was scarce. A Skazerac hunter chased the castaway and lopped off his left arm. (See Chapter VII, above.)

It has been suggested that the Skazerac folk-epic that begins with the lines—

A bunch of the boys were whooping it up down by the Skazerac ice-floe—
actually refers to the famished tribe's ingestion of the hapless castaway's severed limb. According to this interpretation, some of their appetites were not up to it, and "whooping it up" implies the act of regurgitation. (See Partridge, E., A Dictionary of Slang and Unconventional English.)

This interpretation of the folk-epic is especially interesting in light of its sequel, for, according to the Skazerac's oral history, the very same Nameless castaway again landed on their beach many years later, also during an especially lean season.

The tribe knew it was the same man because of his missing arm, though some of its members also debated the significance of his absent right leg. The consensus was that he must be a merciful deity who brought salvation to the faithful by providing sustenance in times of famine. But they also understood that the Wanderer God did not make passive sacrifices. A hunter who was fleet of foot must give chase in order to earn the tribe's reward.

It is told that on this second visit to the Skazeracs, the Wanderer hopped with surprising swiftness and might have escaped had he not run into a great wall of ice where, trapped, he permitted the sacrifice of his other arm (the right one) to the Holy Pursuer.

Immediately thereafter, the castaway began, chipmunk-fashion, to gouge out chunks of ice from the wall that blocked him from the sea. Thus carving himself a passage, he landed back in the freezing ocean, where his new wound was quickly cauterized.

Though the Skazeracs have suffered other times of want, the Wanderer God has not returned a third time. The natives have two schools of thought about why this is so: 1. None of these subsequent times of trial have been of sufficient magnitude to warrant his reappearance. 2. The tribal shamans declare that the Skazeracs have become so lax in the observation of the old customs, totems and rites that they have lost the power to summon their ingestible messiah.

Contemporary theological scholars treat the legend's evolution as a degeneration of Judeo-Christian symbols into a banquet myth devoid of deeper meaning. But whatever the truth behind the legend, every year the Skazeracs still celebrate a sacred "whooping" day.

XVIII

CLOSE ENCOUNTER OF THE WORST KIND

When our Nameless hero found himself, maimed but cauterized, in the chilly ocean, he hoped that the unpredictable currents might cast him up somewhere near Siberia, but it was not to be. Instead, he was washed up on the white sands of the island princessipality of Lesser Britalania.

Greater Britalania, with cash loans and scientific expertise from a truculent eastern power, was trying to become a power to reckon with, and in this pursuit intended to experiment with nuclear weaponry. The first test, scheduled to be held on the southern coastline of Lesser Britalania, was about to take place just as A. Q. Nameless crawled out of the sea.

Astronomers around the world observed him en route to the planet Neptune.

XiX

STAR WHiRLS

Neptune, it is well known in the multiverse, is a swinging water world. Nine-tenths of it is covered with ocean, and the remaining tenth with music shops.

One afternoon, as Johannes Sevastipol Bloch was attempting to sell a left-handed theremin to a farenacean from the Qash! sector of the Veebal Sea, a great crash reverberated from the rear of Bloch's store and deharmonized the air he had been playing as a therastration, as he liked to call it. (The melody was an old burlesque hall rouser Bloch wrote for Lalu Shanna, who used it in her intermingled magic and strip act, in which she produced Neptunian rabbits [remarkably similar to the terrestrial species – Yr. Humble Piescribe] from her garments as she divested them. It was popularly known as Bloch's Hare on a G-String.)

Bloch hurried to the back of his shop and saw a strange person, possibly a Melzafamerian, though he had one less limb than that species usually possesses. The Nameless creature was also hairless, all of it apparently having been singed away.

The creature spoke no recognizable language, so Bloch, pitying him (it?), gave him a room on the second floor and had him enrolled in a remedial Neptunian course where, in a matter of weeks, the hapless visitor at last was able to haltingly communicate with Bloch. "Not that he had much to say. Mostly, after a few words of Neptunian, he'd lapse into his native tongue, repeating the same three words over and over again. There is no precise way to reproduce them in civilized Neptunian." (Very free translation of Bloch's original Neptunian.— Yr. HPS)

At length, Bloch's patience and budget stretched thin, so he made a deal with the government to use his guest as a vital part of a Neptunian space program. Thus the Nameless person was shot into space in the direction of what Neptunians call the Dark World. Samples of Bloch's best music went with him in the ship because the musician had ascertained that his visitor at least knew how to carry a tune.

XX

STAR WHORLS

The furthest planet from Earth— if it is a planet; recent opinion has downgraded its status— is the small globe that Neptunians call the Dark World, though it is better known to terrestrials as Pluto. Unfortunately, the ship that carried A. Q. Nameless looked suspiciously like an elongated bone, as it had been designed by a Neptunian who saw 2001 on his interstellar TV set.

Pluto, therefore, proved hostile to the Nameless spacecraft, A few barks, an aggressive snap— and our protagonist swiftly steered in the opposite direction. Some time and distance later, the ship's fuel ran out, and so did its momentum. It crash-landed on Mars.

XXi

STAR WELLS

When A. Q. Nameless saw the delicate tracery of the mythical canals lining the face of Mars like cosmetics lying about the planet's age, he became so enrapt in the spectacle that he forgot that he was falling toward the red planet. His mind and spirit were transfigured; he remember the paper candy he prized when he was a boy, the red and yellow and blue confections that he ate, paper included, so much over the years as to amount to a sapling. The first shrink he consulted said he had an alder ego.

Suddenly his reverie was abruptly interrupted.

Ouch!

He landed.

Spraying silent siliconian showers in its wake, a desert-sailboat glided noiselessly across the hot sands of Mars. It stopped, and a thin yellow native wearing a badge confronted the Nameless intruder.

"Fingerprints, please."

The immigrant was hard-pressed to satisfy the demand, embarrassed as he was with a dearth of digits. Unfortunately, he learned that without registrable fingerprints, Mars is an unpleasant place to visit. He was relegated to working in the sofva wells, where he fished up sofva seeds for a meager sustenance. He finally obtained special permission from the High Supreme Landlord of Mars, a land developer who lived earthside but passed occasional laws. (His latest dictum rescinded an earlier order that Mars must look exactly like Waukegan, Illinois, in the terrestrial year 1929 A. D.) After several scintillant seasons in the sofva wells, our Nameless hero was told by the H. S. Landlord that he could win his freedom by participating in the upcoming biannual graditorial festival.

XXII

THE COMING OF BATTER TIMES

Hoarse shouts, expelling fetid breaths. The Emperor of Mice Cream raised his thumbs and a sprightly blare of strumpets sounded.

The Nameless immigrant trod on the hot sand, waiting for a massive monster to emerge from the far end of the arena. He was the first of the day's gradiators.

"Hear, O Fingerprintless One!" the Emperor proclaimed. "You are permitted five minutes, no longer, to gradiate yourself to freedom!"

With that, amidst the massed mumbling of myriad masses, a huge cow in a brown vest was released into the amphitheater. Instantly divesting itself of its vest, it swiftly produced eighteen quarts of milk, forty-five tubs of butter, three gallons of vanilla mice cream, a hogshead of uncoddled yogurt, and as a graditorial gesture, a pound of Trappist cheese made by monks who knew how to keep their yaps shut.

The Nameless gradiator, who had prepared for this event with by drilling himself for months, whirled into action. He sampled and tasted and prod his remaining toes into every pit and glob and tub and mucilaginous mess, hopping into every dairy product in a frenzy of cowculation.

The crowd, awestruck, cried,"AWW!" as they heard a flurry of Nameless proclamations at the top of his shrill voice: "Grade A milk! Grade B yogurt! Mice cream... premium grade!" In fifty seconds less than the allotted time, he triumphed and won his victory. The Emperor stuck his thumbs up and the Nameless gradiator was instantly put in a rocket and shipped off to Earth.

XXiii

CHRONOLOGICAL COOKERY

T ime travel, all pundits concur, is a paradox; at best, pure theory. Only the least artless scribe would opt to foist the notion on her or his reader's sensibilities.

Thus, when a certain mechanical space-pod plopped unceremoniously into the palace at Versailles one festive afternoon during the reign of Louis XIV, its Nameless pilot aptly expressed his utmost doubt: "This isn't happening," he declared.

Because he was so positive that what he was witnessing was an impossibility, he displayed no interest in the array of chefs ceremoniously carrying in a huge assortment of comestibles, to which the powered, bewigged, altogether frizzed-up company of nobles fell upon with a voraciousness seemingly at odds with their noble social station.

"This isn't happening," the Nameless itinerant yawned, wondering how to exchange the current scene for something more current.

As the feast drew to a close, four large lackeys wheeled in from the pantry a pastry larger than an SUV. Nameless's ennui suddenly disappeared.

Looks rather like a miniature of my old pie statue, he thought.

"Eh, maintenant, votre Excellence," one of the lackeys intoned, "le pièce de resistance... Gateau a la Siberienne!"

Paradox or not, our Nameless hero instantly decided to credit the occasion with credibility, objective reality, and total veracity. With an ecstatic shriek, he hopped on his sole remaining leg out of his time capsule and smack into the middle of the pie.

Unfortunately, it was not Siberian Peach Pie at all, but a concoction devised by the chief chef, J. Quidnunc Siberienne, thus its name. In actuality, the pastry was filled with school slates; out of the pastry, a conjurer was supposed to emerge and entertain the royalty with a series of amazing magical calculations.

"Mordieux!" the chef exclaimed, then, lapsing into English, his native tongue (Siberienne was fanciful nomenclature; he'd been born Jacob Lipshutz), he howled, "That idiot has ruined my four-and-twenty blackboards bakèd in a pie!"

The conjurer was also broken up by the disaster (a broken arm and a snapped wand).

The Nameless intruder tried to escape, but a company of musketeers seized him and quick-hopped him off to the Bastille, where one of the torturers whittled, "I shall not ruin the King's fun" on his back ten times.

The time machine/space pod was pounded into a collage and hung over Louis's second-best water closet.

XXiV

THE iNEDiBLE UMBRELLA

One day, while traversing Jermyn Street, his garish umbrella in hand, Professor J. Adrian Fillmore (Gad, what a name!), aka James Phillimore, realized he was becoming rather peckish, just as he noticed the façade of a new restaurant: an Italian-French place that called itself The Bridge of Versighs. (The Professor is the protagonist of this author's "Incredible Umbrella" tetralogy. The parasol itself is quite large and garishly colored; pressing its button takes Fillmore wherever he is thinking of, usually some world based on the literature of, e. g., Gilbert & Sullivan land, Shakespeare, etc.)

He grimaced at the pun, but resolved to try their cuisine. But as he made for the door, a tipsy diner emerged and bumped into the Professor, whose thumb inadvertently brushed against the release button of his bumbershoot... and the next thing he knew he stuck his head out of a gigantic pastry.

"Merde!" screamed J. Quidnunc Siberienne. "De nouveau?!"

Thus Fillmore spoiled the chef's second attempt at serving Gateaux Siberienne to Louis XIV. The Professor was promptly popped into a cell in the Bastille, which he was made to share with a somewhat emaciated Nameless prisoner.

The next morning, the pair was gone, umbrella and all.

"May I drop you off someplace?" the Professor asked politely, clinging to his parasol and chattering from the cold of interdimensional space.

His passenger tried to stutter, "Siberia," but Phillimore's mind was preoccupied with finding someplace not chilly. His umbrella, doing its best to interpret his meaning, avoided South America and deposited its Nameless traveler in Darkest Africa. Phillimore, meanwhile, hurried along to his next sequel.

XXV

THE CONGA LINE, OR, LUCKY LINDSAY

Bumlay bumlay bumlay bum
　　　(*PERCUSSIVELY*)
Mumbo-Jumbo, Dance God of the Jungle, is worshipped
By those who skittle hop rap dance prance waddle whoop
　　　and whorf

But mainly they do The Conga
　　　(*MIT SCHLAG*)

One-two-three-HUH
　While out of the jungle
　HopHOPhopHOPhopHOP
　Comes a NAMELESS TRAVELER

(*i*)

　　　　Mumbo-Jumbo sends his priests to investigate
　　　　And they do a chopHUHchopHUH

(*CHANT WHILE WEARING AN OVERCOAT*)

XXVI

MEANWHILE, BACK AT THE ISLE

Further evidence of the persistence of the Skazerac myth in native culture may be perceived in the manner in which the Wandering God pops up in the most unlikely places, such as the African ceremony in which distant (1,875 miles as the ice floes) cousins of the Skazerac nation swear that the Nameless deity visited them just when their island kin were facing another seasonal famine.

The Skazeracs received a parcel (postage due) containing one salt-packed leg (left).

XXVii

LiGHTS OUT!

cene: *Africa, darkest part.*

Sound: boomBOOMboomBOOM etc.[12]

Pitch blackness. Then, after a moment, tiny eyes glow maliciously here and there. Dim shapes of trees, behind which said eyes are busy maliciousing.

Sound: slitherSLITHERslither (N.B.: Do not use snake sounds here.)

ON CAMERA – a strange, half-discernible Nameless shape. Though it appears manlike, it is on all fours (or the remnants of same).

The Nameless Shape is heading north (more or less toward Siberia). The eyes watch the shape's progress.

N. S.

piePIEpiePIEpiePIE (etc.)

---

[12] The producer got a good deal on tom-toms from a local chieftain named Jones who runs a neighboring country. Seems to know a lot about drums.

Suddenly the eyes widen and with many yells, a savage tribe of pygmies leap from behind the trees and seize the N. S. They carry him through the forest howling and screaming and generally behaving indecorously.

XXViii

HOW TO SECURE AN AFRICAN SHRINK

In the middle of the deepest jungle, about fifty miles away from Anywhere and just over the border from Nowhere, there lived a kindly, kingly pygmy named Uggawamma O'Hara. He often had dinner at Hannibal's, the local diner, just across the county line, where he could always find fresh, sweet meat.

But once a minor territorial dispute divided the usually affable neighboring tribes. It happened when a Nameless Stranger was seen crossing the border between the two counties. Hannibal claimed the N. S. belonged to his people, but Uggawamma claimed that the N. S. was his lawful prize. However, in the spirit of conciliation, he offered to relinquish him once he was finished shrinking his head. This did not at all reconcile Hannibal to the plan, for his favorite meal was Tete de Foe. Ultimately, Uggawamma, following the example of Julius Caesar, settled the issue by dividing Hannibal into three parts. After that, the two tribes got along quite peacefully, as did, of course, Hannibal.

Now Ugawamma was an enlightened ruler. He'd studied head-shrinking for months thanks to a correspondence course he'd found by way of The Learning Annex. But rather than slavishly following instructions, he was determined to innovate. And here is the recipe he devised:

2 lbs. river sand, heated
1 Nameless Stranger
Needle and thread
1 Ladle, large
1. Pack river sand into mouth, nose, ears of N. S.
2. Sew up same.
3. Let settle till tender, testing with ladle.
4. Remove thread.

Result: one Nameless Stranger with a head the size of a Ping Pong ball. So deft and delicate was the procedure that the N. S. actually survived the experience.

Unfortunately for the late Hannibal's tribe, who'd been promised the results, said results wriggled free and began a dash to freedom. (To understand how he managed that, see next chapter.)

XXIX

A LAD WHO USED HIS HEAD

T*he scene is a glade in an African forest. Out of his ropes slips a Nameless little man sans limbs with a Ping Pong ball sized head. He begins to flee.*

NAMELESS (*Singing*)

First you put your wee head way up tight;
You swing it your left, you swing it to your right;
You huddle up with all your might,
Then you toss it out just as far as you have sight.
Stretch your little neck way out in space
And do a torso-rock with style and grace.
Repeat once more and wiggle your ass,
And that's what I call an escape with class!

He throws his head forward, scrunches his body to catch up, tosses head again, et cetera, and in this slithery fashion, with astonishing speed, he runs from his clamoring pursuers.

NATIVES (*Singing*)

O, in view of cravings inner,
Let us go and chase our dinner,
Or we shall grow much thinner,
Tra la la.
For our prisoner is fleeing,

A sight we don't like seeing,
For it irks our tribal being,
Tra la la.

NAMELESS (*Singing*)

O, merrily, merrily, I'm running away.
Simply can't tarry. Don't ask. I can't stay.
If I slowed down, I'd sure rue the day.
Pie pie pie pie pie pie pie!
Don't ask me to slacken, don't beg me to stop,
Don't bother to threaten or howl, stamp or hop,
I don't even care if you call a cop.
Pie pie pie pie pie pie pie!

The Nameless quarry escapes. He skirts the edge of a swamp filled with crocogators,[13] but is still not caught.

CROCOGATORS (*Singing*)

Snap! Snap! Snap! Snap! Snap! Snap! Snap!
We tried to catch him in our trap!
A tasty morsel got past our dorsal!
He got away! O, crap, crap, crap!

---

[13] Crocogators are an especially vicious reptile with the head of an alligator on one end of its body, and the head of a crocodile at the other extremity. The perceptive naturalist will surely determine why these beasts are so fierce.

XXX

FROM SEA TO SHINY SEA

A.Q. Nameless travel-slithered a long, exhausting time across the Sahara Desert. His passage was unremarkable, save for one fevered moment when he beheld a mirage: a distant sand dune seemed to him to be an enormous Siberian Peach Pie. But of course it wasn't.

He finally reached the Mediterranean Sea and flopped gratefully into its calm blue waters. As he drifted northward, he murmured to himself, "Seldom [a discouraging word – Yr. Humble Piemage] have I allowed myself to think I would ever get this close!" Which shows, of course, how relative the concept of distance can be to those who are truly desperate. Eventually, after a long, uneventful drift, our Nameless hero washed up on a Turkish beach, where he was discovered by none other than Abe Grandbody, an expatriate from Pismo Beach.

"Gevalt!" quoth Grandbody. "This is truly déja vu!" He lovingly deposited his find at the Home for Turkish Delights (mostly inhabited by blind patients). There our Nameless flotsam recuperated and eventually squiggled off northward past a goodly gaggle of goose farms. As he cut cross country, he was reminded of Kentucky, though here all the straw he saw was in Turkey, not the opposite.

At last he reached the Black Sea, which he prompty rolled into and perambuswam towards its northern shore, which, he knew was the gateway to—

Yes!

SIBERIA!!!

XXXi

THE MOSCOW CONNECTiON

At curtain rise, in the distance is heard the twang of a breaking jews-harp. As the sound dies away, VASHA, PASHA and TRASHA all sigh. They are brothers and dearly love each other. At the beginning, they are all juggling billiard balls.

VASHA

Oy, oy, oy, what a life!

PASHA

What a world!

TRASHA

When I was fourteen, I used to bathe in the Volga, and the boatmen would shout Volga things at me. But it was a very good year.

VASHA

Eight ball in the side pocket!

PASHA

If only Mama would take us to Moscow.

TRASHA

But we're already in Moscow!

PASHA

I'm talking Moscow, Pennsylvania.

TRASHA

When I was fifteen, I shot wild strawberries on the steppes. It was a very good year.

VASHA

That was wrong of you. You shouldn't shoot nothing you don't intend to eat.

TRASHA

Not even with a camera?

PASHA

He can't eat strawberries. They give him a rash.

TRASHA

Not always.

VASHA

Y'see? You should never make rash statements.

Their old NURSE enters.

NURSE

Little ones, play nice. Want a drop of wodka?

TRASHA

When I was sixteen, you pronounced that word with a "wee." It was a lousy year.

NURSE

You're such a cute little wise-mouth!
(*She kicks him in the crotch and exits.*)

TRASHA

Oy, oy, oy, what a life!

PASHA

It could be worse.

VASHA

How?

PASHA

Something could happen.

VASHA

When I was seventeen, something happened. But I forget what.

Enter PLOTZO and SHLOCKY, carrying luggage.

PLOTZO

Halt, Shlocky!

Shlocky slavers, and halts, but does not set down the bags.

PASHA

Why does he slaver so much?

PLOTZO

You want to know why he is slavering? He's slavering because he's a Slav!

VASHA

I'm bored.

TRASHA

When I was eighteen, I was bored. I still am. Let's go.

PASHA

We can't.

VASHA

Why not?

PASHA

We're waiting.

PLOTZO

Who are you waiting for? (*No answer*) What are you waiting for? (*No answer*) Why are you waiting? (*No answer*) How are you waiting? (*No answer*) When I don't have to ask. You're waiting now. That much I figured out. The rest is silence. I quote.

PASHA

Allow me to elucidate.

TRASHA

When I was nineteen, there was a day when I elucidated.

VASHA

Liar! You're not nineteen ye... you're eighteen and three quarters.

TRASHA

You're calling me a liar?!

He kicks VASHA in the crotch. The three brothers fight each other.

PLOTZO

O, I say, this IS diverting! Isn't it Shlocky?

SHLOCKY

Diverting begirting exerting fa-flirting ha-hurting...

PLOTZO

O, shut up and slaver!

The brothers stop fighting.

VASHA

So why doesn't he put down his bags?

PLOTZO

Why don't you ask him?

Vasha begins to ask SHLOCKY, but stops when SHLOCKY kicks his crotch..

Suddenly a Nameless person enters in an odd and slithery manner. He asks a question no one hears.

OMNES

WHAT?

NAMELESS PERSON

(*Shouting*) I asked which way is Siberia?

They all point in different directions.

Thanks!

He slithers merrily out, sure he is headed correctly.

PLOTZO

That's all the significance I can tolerate for today. I'm going. (*He does not move.*)

TRASHA

Maybe I'll go, too. (*He does not move.*)

PASHA

Who was that pinball-headed stranger?

NAMELESS PERSON

(*Off*) Hiyo, pie!

VASHA

Tomorrow we'd better sell the peach orchard.

The curtain does not move.

XXXii

SO CLOSE!

Now when our Nameless hero at last slithered across the vast wastes of Mother Russia, he at long long long long last found himself in Siberia.

YES! You read that right, sonnyevitch... SIBERIA!!!

As he made his tortuous way along the rail lines that he was following he saw a long line of fifty or more bolsheviks riding along, spitting at the peasants and shouting, "Hail Stalin! Down with the Capitalists!"

At that very moment, A. Q. Nameless espied a sign.

Ye Sign:

SIBERIA RESTAURANT
Still Cooler Inside!

Joyfully, he headed (literally) in that direction, but as he did, the mighty line of bolsheviks suddenly cried Haltski! to their hoarses, which had been trotski-ing.

The leader of the force shouted, "Hey, Nameless Strangernik!"

"What?" the Nameless one asked in a tiny voice.

"You've got a head the size of a Ping Pong ball! You must be a spy!"

They promptly arrested him and threw him in jail.

XXXiii

VATHEK THE HELL?
OR, DIS MUS' BE DE BLACE!

t chanced that the cell in which our Nameless hero was thrust was shared by several other prisoners. To while away the time of their respective incarcerations, they collectively agreed to unfold their various histories to one another.

The first to speak was a former journalist, W. Windchill Factor. With a sigh, he embarked upon his sorrowful tale…

"Once upon a time," quoth he, "I was a lowly streetcar conductor, but I was really lousy at my job, so, possessing no other viable talents, I drifted into journalism and became a well-known reporter; I had a syndicated column, and broadcast live on radio and TV. Once I got hot on a story about some Nameless boob who, I concluded, had some kind of pie fetish. My theory about him was so incredible that my boss refused to let me broadcast it. We argued, tempers flared, and he finally tried to fire me, but I beat him to it… with a .22 slug. Well, they threw me in jail, and I was convicted and sent to Death Row.

"But I had a smart attorney named Fogg, of the old firm of Dodson Jr. and Fogg III. He appealed my case. The case was deliberated in the State Supreme Court, but Fogg lost and I was sent back to Death Row. That's when Dodson Jr. stepped in. He has enormous clout, which is a polite way to say he's a master of graft. He appealed my case to the Supreme Court! It dragged on a long while— "

"And you finally won?" one of the other prisoners asked.

"Nope. They agreed I should be parboiled. It's a shame, too, because I was just about to sell my book, How to Shoot Your Boss and Win! Anyway, they finally got me onto the hot seat and the executioner pulled the switch."

He paused for effect, and one of his Nameless prison-mates promptly asked if that meant he was therefore dead.

"But nay," Factor replied, a little horse from all the talking. "They hit me with all the juice they could send through me, but it didn't hurt at all. They couldn't put me in jeopardy a second time, so my attorneys tried to get the President to commute my sentence to life imprisonment, but the Justice Department was so embarrassed by the whole botched job that they got the State Department to enroll me in a prisoner exchange program with Russia, so here I am."

"Interesting story," one of the other prisoners commented. "Did they eventually discover some sort of malfunction in the electric chair?"

"Absolutely not," the journalist demurred. "You should pay closer attention when a famous professional talks to you. Didn't I begin by explaining that I started my career as a really lousy conductor?"

They all went to sleep much edified.

XXXiV

CAESARIAN SECTION

R ecently," said the next inmate, "a thing happened to me
that was so awful I fled my native land, only to end up
here where I was arrested for being stupid."

"It's a crime to be stupid?" the Nameless prisoner
squeaked.

"When you're as dumb as this guy," W. Windchill
Factor nodded, "believe me, it's a crime. I know his story
because I was still a big deal newspaperman and got to write
the story about him when he almost got killed."

The inmate in question gestured for Factor to
continue. "I'm sure you'll tell it better than me, so go ahead."

So Factor did.

"Jason Grimslaugh Ytansebea Nilding was the
improbable name of the richest, nastiest miser in Happy
Valley, Kansas, where that poor sap sitting over there grew up.
Nilding was so wealthy his compound interest was an unlisted
number. He invested in a lot of unsavory ventures, including
rum-running, drug-dealing, and coke-bottling. He was in such
ill repute in his own family that while he was alive he was
frostily ignored by his spinster sisters Matilda Waltzing and
Julia Swagman, Australians who changed their names so no
one would associate them with their disgraceful brother."

The journalist pointed to the inmate whose story he
was telling. "Now this young dolt was Nilding's nephew, and
he worked as caretaker on his uncle's estate. When the old
man died, no one knew where all of his ill-earned capital was.
He'd often boasted that he'd hidden it somewhere safe from

all prying eyes, familial or governmental. He did write a will, and it stipulated that the money would only be shared equally by his two sisters if they kept his businesses going. If not, they were free to roam the grounds and try to find out where his fortune was hidden. But the will also contained a warning— there was a curse on the hiding place."

The narrator shrugged. "Well, of course Matilda and Julia refused to have anything to do with their late brother's criminal activities. They felt it only proper that his blood money be found and donated to a worthy cause.'

"This is where I come in!" the prisoner who'd once been a caretaker boasted.

Factor cast an eloquently piteous look at him, then continued. "Yes, this is where he comes in. The two ladies got in touch with this dimbulb and said that if he found out where his uncle's fortune was hidden, they'd buy him a T-shirt. So he began searching every room in the mansion, but found nothing, He ripped open all of the furniture, but the answer was, as they say in this place, nyet. He dug everywhere over the whole thirty-acre estate. Zilch! Finally there was only place he had not checked out. Would you like to tell them where?"

The prisoner grinned. "The place the old guy was buried!"

"Ah, yes," the narrator nodded, "the burial vault itself. We ran a photo of it in the newspaper— it was enormous! Imagine a massive granite tombstone with a carving of the old miser on it showing him counting his ill-gained shekels. Well, this stupid idiot here totally ignored the will's warning and started digging. He didn't even stop when a recording clicked on and his uncle's voice said, 'I wouldn't do that if I were you!' But he just kept on digging, until he finally got to the coffin, pried it open and indeed found, along with the mouldering bones, a huge amount of jewelry, stocks, bonds, cash in large denominations, and ten pounds of Spanish fly lollipops.

"The dullard was delighted. He'd earned his T-shirt. But then the timer in the coffin set off the curse, no supernatural thing, you see— an engineering feat that blew up the whole mansion. The explosion knocked over the gravestone and it banged brainless here on the noggin. A second explosion fire-stormed all the loot into ash, and hurled the caretaker a quarter mile or so into the sky. He landed and an ambulance rushed him to the hospital, but since his major injury was the blow the gravestone administered to his thick head, he managed to recover."

"But I was so upset," the prisoner mumbled, "I left the country. And here I am, arrested."

"You certainly are arrested," sneered W. Windchill Factor.

"An amazing story!" our Nameless hero declared. "Hard to believe, though!"

"It's absolutely true!" the other declared. He scrabbled in his pocket and brought out a strip of newspaper. "See? I've still got the article Mr. Factor wrote about me!"

"Ah, yes," the journalist proudly declared. "One of my finest columns. I'm particularly fond of the title that I gave it … " And here he read out the headline:

DOWAGERS SHY A HOUSE AND CRIMES;
The Grave Butts Dunce

The prisoners slept soundly that night. It was winter and the bedbugs all were hibernating.

XXXV

THE PASHA'S PECULIAR PASSION
(in memory of Fredric Brown)

O
ne of the prisoners was clad in the colorful garb of an Arabian potentate. "Yes," he said, when asked, "I am the direct descendant of Mustafa Musselman McMullins. How I got here is quite uninteresting, but the tale of my illustrious ancestor is still told in my homeland."

"Which is where?" W. Windchill Factor inquired.

"Tunisia," he replied. "now let me tell you his story." Which he did.

"Two odd predilections governed my great forefather's life. The first was a mania for alliteration, which harmed no one, but the second proved his downfall. Yet there is never anything sour without some complementary sweet, and thus the western world hath inherited a cherished institution out of Mustafa's melancholy misfortune.

"He was the High and Huffy Hotshot, Primordial Pasha and Divine Dey of the medium-ancient land of Tunisia. It was well known to his subjects and servants that he passed much of his time consuming condiment-covered culinary concoctions. He doted on swordfish stew laced with marshmallow mustard; he lavished encomiums o'er many a platter of salmon shirred with chocolate catsup, and many were the paeans he composed upon the theme of thyme-and-tulip tea mulled with raspberry relish.

"So obsessed was he with the fulfillment of his fancy feasts that he frequently dispatched a friendly neighborhood sorceress on forays forward in time to find superfluous savories from the far-fetched future. But it was a mistake of a different sort that brought disaster to the hapless pasha.

"Tunisia, you see, often itself embroiled in bitter border brouhaha with the neighboring Queandom of Tripoli, which a long time later became the capital of Libya. For a while, an uneasy peace existed between the two countries, but the situation changed when two twin sisters took over the Tripolitan government.

"Lydia and her sibling Phydia, according to their political detractors, learned the art of the court by beginning their careers as courtesans. Whether there was any truth to the tale, who can say? Certainly those who started the rumor were never consulted about their source, but that's because they were swiftly executed when the twins came to power, which event occurred immediately after the demise of their predecessor in their twinned arms.

"To stave off further talk and possible revolution, the young women resurrected the old Tunisian border battle in order to distract their subjects with a foreign scapegoat. Pasha Mustafa's minions murmured that he should seek some kind of compromise, but he licked the mayonnaise and mullet from his mustache and roared, 'Never shall Mustafa stoop so low as to harangue with harlots!'

"Now despite his prandial preoccupations, Mustafa had actually long studied the Tunisian-Tripolitan boundary debate. 'The primary problem,' he declared to his courtiers, 'is a paucity of professional paraphernalia for properly pinpointing problematic parameters.'

"And with that, he summoned the sorceress. Her name was Hecate Hallelu Halloran, late of Babbleonia. She lived on a small isle near the pasha's palace. Though she was never one of his servile servants, early in his reign she agreed to form an alliance with him, mostly because she found it fun to find new philosophies to fiddle with during her fore-flights to obtain overlardings for Mustafa's meals.

"Lately, Hecate had been spending time investigating Sino-solipsism and was especially enamored of that branch of Buddhism devoted to intuition and introspection. Indeed, when Mustafa spoke the spell which specified the search for sophisticated surveying stuff, she was in her study singing 'OM,' while subduing a screaming six-hundred-pound Japanese wrestler she'd stolen on her last safari. Because she was enjoying herself, she did not rush to fulfill the pasha's request, a delay that decidedly doomed the distracted dey.

"Mustafa was distracted because the border war was in full fling. While Hecate stayed to drown her opponent's groans with her universal drone, the pasha straddled the imprecise boundary between Tunisia and Tripoli and fired off foul effusions at his nemeses, the putative prostitutes turned tyrants Lydia and Phydia. In turn, they hurled horrible hostilities right back at him.

"Battle tactics turned toward brickbats: the enemies expelled elaborate effluents at one another— firecrackers and fishheads, stale scones and shrimpstalks, cockleshells and cockroaches and the collected criticism of John Simon.

"Summoning their supreme strength, the sisters viciously slung at Mustafa all ten acts of Dryden's The Conquest of Granada. He staggered beneath that horrid slop d'oeuvre and sought to retaliate with something even worse, but alas! nothing was at hand other than a double dipperful of the dinner he'd been meaning to feed his collection of pampered felines. A poor retaliation, perhaps, but he flung it recklessly in the direction of the dreadful duo.

"Unfortunately, just at that moment, Hecate appeared, her arms laden with anachronistic surveyor's levels, crosses, telescopes and a pushbutton-retractable steel tape measure to which she'd taken a personal fancy. The sour-scented catly comestibles smacked her square in the center of her puss.

"The witch whirled wildly on the pasha. 'Swinish ingrate!' she shrieked. 'And did you dare to call me from the howls of mantra-sumo to the whores of Tripoli to fight your country's battles by playing this trick on me? O, my revenge shall be swift! O, cursèd ever shall this first day of the fourth month be till the end of all time!' And with that, Hecate pointed her steel tape measure— the likes of which had never been seen before— at the unhappy pasha. Flames flared forth from its tip and the ruler razed the ruler.

"Yet, as I said earlier, sweet ever stems from sour. And this, I think, will interest our journalist friend, Mr. Factor — for had Mustafa's peculiar passion not led him to smear cat sup on his Tunis-allied Zen witch, the world might never have seen the historically-significant banner headline that appeared the following morning on the front page of The Medium Ancient Times.

"Yes, yes?" Factor asked eagerly. "What did it say?"

"The First Tape Rule Fuels Dey."

XXXVi

BONE APPETiT
(A Yuletide Tail)

Well," said A. Q. Nameless, "who wants to go next?"

They all said they wanted to go.

A friendly neighborhood guard explained why that was not possible. After they all came to, a rangy chap who said he was Canadian spoke up.

"My name is Rudolph," he said. "I once was wealthy, though eventually I squandered it all away. Shall I tell you how I made my fortune?"

"NO!" they all shouted.

"Good," he nodded. "Once upon a time... "

In a secluded sector of the deep north woods, where men are bold and nights are cold, there once lived a trapper with his wife, mother, and a rather nervous crimson-colored dachshund named Rover, who always had to be coaxed into crossing the living-room floor to his food-dish in the far corner. ("Red Rover, red Rover, come over," his owner would repeatedly insist.)

The trapper's name was Rudoph Woods, and his wife was the former Marsha Titwillow of the Arcadian Titwillows: a comely lass of twenty-four (it was a very large family). Marsha owned a cool $24,000,000, lawfully inherited from her unlawful grandfather, the maple baron of Crooked Cove.

Her husband did not have $24,000,000. As his wife frequently reminded him, he did not even have $0.24. It perturbed him to the point where he involved himself in all sorts of get-rich-quick schemes, much to the detriment of his wife's temper, though not her inexhaustible bank account. His ego, forever frustrated by his spouse's fortune, sought justification in self-improvement: he took correspondence courses galore till he was the most accomplished correspondent in Saskabaskatraz. With his skills, he earned a pittance writing letters for the Mayor. (His Honor's favorites were Q and T; his official actions often required them.)

Woods first met Ms. Titwillow while working on her carburetor, which he fancied. She found this a novel experience. Many months later, they declared their nuptial vows. Disillusion swiftly followed. Not only did she divest herself of her carburetor, but she made his life a living hell. It all began the first night they settled into the Titwillow family home in the great northern woods.

Dinnertime. Rudy contemplated his first home-cooked meal with relish (Indian). Plucking his napkin from its ring, he took knife and fork in hand and waited while his wife placed a covered platter upon the table and lifted its lid...

Turning his nose up at the odor emanating from the grey mass piled high on the great plate, he asked, "What is that?"

"A recipe I got from Mrs. Broderick's mother. She hasn't been feeling well."

"What is it?" he repeated.

"Probably arthritis."

'No, I mean what's that on the plate?"

"A recipe I got from Mrs. Broderick's mother."

"What do you call it?"

"Arthritis, I think."

"Marsha!"

She shrugged. "Oh, you mean dinner. Call it goulash."

He eyed the food suspiciously. "Sure doesn't look like goulash."

"I didn't say it was. I said, call it goulash... if you like."

He speared a small portion, brought it to his mouth and chewed it. The revolted trapper grimaced. "It sure doesn't taste like goulash."

"That's because it's liver."

He blanched. "I hate liver!"

"Nonsense, it's good for you. It's full of protein and keeps you healthy. I've eaten it all my life and I'm sound as a brand-new car!"

"Without a carburetor," he grumbled.

"Well, get used to it, buster," Marsha said, "because it's the only meat we can afford on your income."

"What about your money? You could afford better food than liver!"

"Bosh!" she scoffed. "I like liver. Be glad. You've got a wife who is happy to live within your meager budget. Don't be ungrateful."

"I'm not ungrateful," he protested. "Just hungry."

"Then eat your liver."

He threw down his napkin and stormed to the larder, but the cupboard was bereft of anything except liver. Canned. Dried. Chopped. Minced. Liver paste. Liver salt. He looked in the icebox. Liver cutlets. Iced liver pie. Liversicles.

He sighed and sat back down at the table. He choked down some of his dinner, while his wife ate it all and had second helpings.

After dinner, she read her spouse one of her favorite poems.

The Bridge to the Liver Pies

O, you may have your rainbow
And it's bright golden pot,
But if I could, I would go
Unto a place I'm not—

It was an iron bridge-way,
'Twas not much for the eyes
But at its latter end lay
Two rabbit-liver pies.

'Twas high up in the Andes
Some miles above the seas:
All circled round by candies
And chocolate cherry freeze!

But as I neared the bridgework,
A green and orange troll
Cried, "Halt right there, my good jerk,
Unless you've got the toll!"

I did a smart about-face,
Although my tear-ducts burned
And no more did I retrace
My steps once I'd returned.

O, I have roamed the world wide
Where wonders stun the eyes,
But nowhere have I spied
A marvel like those pies!

It's not the bridge's pass-fee
That keeps me from my goals…
It's just that fine folk like me
Don't talk to common trolls!

Later that month, Rudolph moaned, "What am I going to do?" as he gulped down his twentieth plate of liver noodle casserole. "Liver at every meal, and nothing else to eat." At that moment, he noticed something under the table nudge his leg. He looked down and saw his shy dog, Rover, cowering, afraid, as usual, to cross the room and eat his dinner. Woods lowered his plate stealthily to let his pet help itself to the unwanted liver casserole. To his dismay, Rover suddenly conquered his customary diffidence and dashed over to his own supper-dish, which he gratefully assayed.

Marsha surveyed the scene frostily. She'd seen it all. "Lile master, like dog," she sneered. "Neither one of you would know good food if you fell on it."

It occurred to Rudolph that such an action might at least improve the casserole's texture, but he wisely refrained from voicing the thought.

That winter, the north woods suffered the Great Blizzard of '69. Things, already bleak in the Woods household, got even worse. Rover avoided his master now, afraid he might be forced to share his dinner. Rudy grew paler and thinner.

At the height of the snowstorm, they were totally cut off from town. The trapper grew so bored that he even went upstairs sometimes to chat with his mother, Mamalah Smambo (she'd kept her maiden name).

"So?" she greeted her son, "have you got your mitts on her cash yet?"

He shook his head.

"Then bug off, loser."

"Look, Mama, food's running low. There's only about two hundred pounds of liver left in the icebox."

"Suits me. I don't like the stuff."

"Neither do I."

"Sure," she shrugged, "but it's free."

"But I HATE IT!"

"So eat snow," his mother suggested.

Her idea surprised him. To his liver-besotted brain, the notion sounded positively appealing.

"Thanks, Ma! I will!" And he rushed downstairs and out of the house.

Fried snow. Baked snow. Broiled snow. The possibilities were endless.

It was definitely better than liver, he decided. Still, something was lacking ... what was it?

It was hard to remember the word. Savor? No— flavor! That was the word!

He turned his efforts to trying to amend the flavor problem. But the next morning, the solution came from an unexpected direction.

"Rudy!" his wife said, shaking a finger in his face, "you have got to talk to that old battleax!"

"Who?"

"Your mother!"

"Why?"

"She says she's bored. So she decided to start raising pets."

"Why not? I've got a dog, so—"

"I wouldn't mind another dog. But she's raising mice."

"Mice?" He thought about it for a moment. "Mice?"

"You heard me. Stop that drooling!"

But later on, in the evening, while Marsha and Rover and Rudy's mother were all asleep, Rudy crept in his parent's room and an hour later, in the kitchen, he cooked his first plate of mouse marinated in snow sauce. It's savory scent wafted upstairs, woke Marsha and Mamalah. Soon they joined him, and even Marsha admitted it was a welcome change in cuisine, though she did wonder what mouse liver might be like as a paté spread on Saltines.

It is a fact of economic note that the appearance of the Woods line of canned mouse-meat occurred during the Great Blizzard of '69. Trundling from one snowbound cottage to another, the trapper – now entrepreneur – dug out his neighbors and nourished them with samples that his family pitched in to make.

Woods's mother, who had a way with the rodents, started a mouse farm right on the estate, and they all hand-packed the comestibles in pure north woods snow, marketing the product in cans with quaint labels bearing a likeness of Mamalah herself on them. The product was named MAMA'S MOUSE.

The oddest detail of Woods's success story is how he raised the funds to erect a cannery factory. All of the components were ordered by mail and dropped by helicopter next to the still-snowbound estate. The cost was roughly $35,000.

Where did the impoverished businessman get the money?

His wife actually advanced it to him, but on one condition: that he eat her liver dinners without any further fuss. "And that goes for your little dog, too!" she shrilled.

Reluctantly, the would-be millionaire agreed.

" —and that's how I built my fortune," Woods told his fellow inmates in the Russian prison cell.

"But how did you lose it so fast?" asked W. Windchill Factor, always hungry for scandal. "I covered your story for one of the wireless services, and I remember that you lost your company practically overnight."

"That's true," the trapper admitted sadly. "My wife foreclosed on the loan."

"But why? Didn't you keep your part of the bargain?"

"Mr. Factor, I did what I could. I ate the damned liver. But there was no way I could force Rover to do the same."

"Hmmph. I would have forced the mutt."

"Believe me, I tried. I pampered him. I gave him whirlpool baths. I told him dog stories at bedtime. I even sang him to sleep. At Christmas, I actually made up a Carol and worked his name into the lyrics, but nothing worked!"

"A Christmas Carol?" A. Q. Nameless said. "Do you remember it?"

"I certainly do. I wrote it as a commercial for our company." Humming a familiar tune, he sang, *"Rover eats liver with Rudy Woods, to can Mama's Mouse in snow… "*

XXXVii

TALE OF THE POOR SHARECROPPER

Five prisoners, which tally includes our Nameless hero, had not yet spoken. One of them was a black gentleman named Amos, who said he came from the American South. "Never had any luck," he said, "and here's proof... I came over here as a tourist, misplaced my papers, and here I am. But once a long time back, my luck changed, at least for a little while, and here's how it happened... "

Amos lived on a soil-poor tract of land in the deep South with his feisty wife Amanda. She sent him out in all sorts of weather to work, no matter whether he felt good or bad. They had no children, and that's because she never allowed her undernourished, timid husband anywhere near her bed.

One dreary day, Amos awoke feeling very hungry. Amanda was having ham-hocks and eggs from breakfast, but there was nothing left for him.

"That looks good," he said wistfully.

"It is, but you're not getting any."

"I'm sure hungry. I didn't eat last night, and last morning all I had was leavings from the night before."

Amanda looked at him with a little bit of pity. "Well, Amos, if you'll just pick up that ol' shotgun, and roam the woods, I reckon you can shoot us some game that I will cook for you."

So Amos picked up his rusty rifle that only had a few bullets left in it, and roamed along the dry, cracked land between his shack and the muddy river, but he could not find any game. Nothing… not even a sparrow.

After a while, he crossed the river, wading through its shallows, but couldn't even spot a catfish in it. Along the dusty countryside he trudged. Woods loomed up in the distance. Thinking he might be luckier there, he entered them, but saw no game, not even a rabbit or a squirrel.

The sun baked him, parching his throat and cracking his skin. Far off, though, he saw a tiny cloud, dark as could be, no bigger than the fist of a baby girl-child. But the cloud drifted nearer and nearer and as it did, the wind began to come up and cool his sweating brow. The closer the cloud got, the larger, darker, and more ominous it looked until—

WHAM! SIZZLEBAM! BANG!

Lightning and thunder burst over the head of poor, cowering Amos. A deluge of rain slashed down, ruining every hope he had of finding game or making his decrepit weapon work. It was a merciless cold downpour that soaked him through and through and brought with it a serious case of the shivers and shakes.

Amos scurried through the woods, trying to find some drier spot to wait out the storm. He found a tree and huddled beneath it, wet and miserable. Only his aching feet were glad of the rainwater puddling where he stood, for he'd walked a great distance that day, maybe twenty miles, and now it was getting dark, and there was no chance of getting home that night, not that Amanda would worry the least bit over his absence. Maybe, Amos thought, the best thing he could do would be to lay right down beneath the tree and let the waters close over him.

But as the rain continued to pelt him, and the sun went away and left him in the dark, Amos thought he saw, way in the distance and even deeper in the forest, the flickering warm glow of a candle. He worried that it might be ol' will-o-wisp fixing to lure him into quicksand. But then he reckoned it didn't matter much if he survived the night or not, he'd probably die of hunger, anyway, so out of a last desperate resolve, Amos began to slog through the loamy mud, darting from tree to streaming tree. The light grew brighter. After a long sloppy time through the forest, Amos got close enough to see that it was indeed a candle burning bright and cheery on the windowsill of a small, sturdily built wooden cabin, which was raised several feet above the swampy earth by stout hardwood posts driven deep into the ground.

Amos stepped forward and shyly rapped at the front door. No answer. He tried again, a little louder, and this time he heard someone within coming to the door.

The portal opened wide and a friendly eye peered out at him. "Why, you poor soul," he heard a warm, deep woman's voice say, "what are you doing out there in the wet?"

He stammered out his story, how he'd been searching all day for game in the dry fields, but finally got caught in the storm in the forest and was cold and hungry.

The door creaked open. There stood the handsomest honey-eyed gal he'd ever set eyes upon. "Soul," she said, "I'll be honest with you. If what you say is true, then put that ol' rifle down and take off that sopping hat and stay for supper, and get dry before you go back home. If you are a gentleman, you will respect a widow lady and take the charity that is offered you, and do her no harm."

Amos allowed that there was not an ounce of mischief in him, and he was so hungry, anyway, that he had no strength to be anything but good. His timid manner charmed his hostess, so she got an old blanket and held it for him to wrap himself inside while he took off his wet clothes. When he was dry and warmer, she served up supper.

Well, there were ham-hocks and black-eyed peas swimming in butter, cornpone with redeye gravy, turnip greens, coffee and sweet potato pie. He ate like he would be able to carry an extra ration in his stomach. Finally, he pushed away his plate, sighed with weary contentment and tried to thank her mightily, but halfway through what he tried to say, his head nodded onto the tabletop and he dozed off.

She shook his shoulder gently. "Soul," she said, "you can't sleep here. I'm a good, honest woman and you have to be on your way, lest the Devil work his temptations." But even as she spoke, she pitied the poor man, who could hardly open his eyes, and when he pleaded that he would be no trouble, if he could only just rest up that night because it was still too stormy to go home, she sighed and fixed up a pallet for him by the stove. His clothes were still too damp to put back on, so Amos curled up in the blanket she'd given him, and put his head down on a bag of straw she gave him for a pillow.

Funny thing, though, how, in spite of the weariness of his limbs, Amos couldn't quite get back to sleep. His hostess turned down her own bed and blew out the candle by the window, so that the only remaining light came from the stove, as it cast off flickering shadows along the wall. Through lidded eyes, Amos saw her in the semi-darkness strip off her clothing and don her night-things. A fine figure of a woman, he thought, then told himself to forget about it and go to sleep. Which he earnestly tried to do.

Time passed. The rain slacked off to a whisper. An old banjo clocked ticked away the seconds and the minutes. He heard her turn over and sigh. Once. Twice. Fifteen minutes ticktocked away, and again she turned restlessly.

"Excuse me, ma'am," Amos meekly said at last, "are you still awake?"

"That I am," she said suspiciously. "What's troublin' you?"

"I'm only thinkin' that it's dark and quiet an' nobody knows we're here and this ol' pallet is kinda scratchy and the floor is cold, but a big warm ol' bed like that would sure feel fine on my poor ol' bones… "

"Soul!" she snapped, rearing up her head. "I took you in an' fed you an' let you get warm, and I told you I am a good, honest woman and out of the goodness of my heart, I let you stay in the same room with me overnight, but here you go and make me an indecent proposal! I ought to toss your ungrateful butt out into the woods and let you drown!"

Amos stammered his apologies. "Ma'am, now ma'am, I didn't mean nothing wrong! I 'pologize! Seems to me this floor is warmin' up, an' this ol' pallet is startin' to feel real comfy, so I'm satisfied the way I is!"

"Well," she grunted, "let's see that you stay satisfied!" She turned over in bed to go to sleep.

Poor Amos cuddled himself up into a tight ball on his pallet, and soon his weary limbs made their demands and finally he drifted into a deep, dreamless slumber.

The woman lay on her large soft bed and also tried to doze, but by now she was wide awake. She listened to the whisper of the rain taptapping on the logs of the roof and walls. She heard the banjo clock chime the hour. One a. m. One-fifteen. Still she couldn't rest. She said herself six Hail Marys, but it did not help.

One-thirty. Amos snored contentedly. She sat up in bed and recited the Lord's Prayer.

Two a. m. She repeated it for the fortieth time.

At two-fifteen, she turned in his direction, and noticed the blanket where it had fallen away from his small frame. She saw that height had nothing to do with this man's stature.

At two-thirty, just as the banjo clock chimed softly in the darkness, she stuck her legs over the edge of the bed and stretched one of them across the floor until her foot nudged Amos's shoulder. She rocked him till he roused.

"Oh, hell, soul!" she breathed. "You talked me into it!"

XXXVIII

A DECIDEDLY SHAGGY CHAPTER

Four more inmates of the Russian prison had not yet spoken, of which one was our Nameless hero, while another was an odd chap who looked remarkably like said personage, as well as a taciturn Middle-European gent. The last of this quartet was a suntanned sport who introduced himself as Abraham Grandbody.

"I used to be a lifeguard," he declared, "but I have never cared to talk about myself for, in truth, the only times I ever thought I was involved in anything whatever interesting were when I found a certain strange Nameless object washed up on the beach where I was employed." He paused and looked at A. Q. Nameless quizzically.

"However," he resumed, "I have ever and always been a devotee of a sort of humor that may well be a bit abstruse, but of which I have long been a student. Yet before I discuss its nature, allow me to offer a preliminary example of what I intend to expound thereupon—

"To wit," said Grandbody, "have you heard about the three men who all lived in penthouse of a building that was forty-five stories tall? One day, they were on their way home when they found, to their dismay, that the elevator was, as they say, on the fritz, so they decided that they would walk all the way up to their lofty living quarters, but to pass the time as they did, the first of the trio offered to sing songs as they climbed the initial fifteen stories.

"Prominent amongst those he sang was one about Old Grogan's Goat, also known as Old Hogan's Goat. At which point, Abe Grandbody sang:

Old Grogan's goat was feeling fine,
He ate three red shirts off my line.

CHORUS
I ain't a-gonna feed that goat no more! (*Repeat thrice*)

I took a stick, and broke his back,
And tied him to the railroad track! (*Repeat*)

CHORUS
I ain't a-gonna feed that goat no more! (*Repeat thrice*)

A speeding train was coming nigh…
Old Grogan's goat was doomed to die! (*Repeat*)

CHORUS
I ain't a-gonna feed that goat no more! (*Repeat thrice*)

Old Grogan's goat, with a lick o' paint,
Coughed up those shirts, and flagged down that train! (*Repeat*)

CHORUS
I guess I'm gonna feed that goat some more! (*Repeat twice*)

Grandbody also sang about three men lost in the woods who had one log of bologna amongst them, so they decided to go to sleep and let whichever of them had the best dream eat the bologna. And he sang, more or less to the tune of "Pop Goes the Weasel":

Two sons of Erin and a Jew
Went out for recreation,
But they got lost inside the woods,
It ruined their vacation!
They felt so sad, they all were scared,
The night was dark and lonely,
The only food they had with them
Was one piece of baloney.
But one of them put down his blade
And said, "It's no use carving!
For if we share, there's not that much,
We all will end up starving!"
"Well, let us all just go to sleep!"
Suggested old Maloney.
"Whoever has the finest dream
Will eat the baloney!"
The next day, all three got up,
A quarter after seven,
And Patrick said, "I had a dream,
I died and went to Heaven!
St. Peter met me at the gate,
Riding on a pony.
Well, that's a dream that can't be beat!
So I'll eat the baloney!"
"Now hold it, lad," the other said,
"I dreamed of matrimony!
I wed an angel in the sky!
So I get the baloney!"
Their friend, he said, "Oy vey, it's true,
I vatched you both, ven sleeping.
The tings you say, I know are true,
Because, vell, I was peeping ...
And both of you, the angels took,
I felt so sad and lonely!
I thought you'd not come back again ...
So I ate the baloney!"

"Now the second of the three men who shared the penthouse," Abe Grandbody continued, "said that he would divert his climbing companions from floors sixteen through thirty by telling them amusing stories.

One of them concerned a Sultan who was shipwrecked with his Jester and every day at sunset, he would go to the seashore and pray, "O Allah, send me my harem," so the Jester would tell him funny stories till he cheered up, yet every day at sunset, the Sultan still would go to the seashore and pray, "O Allah, send me my harem," so the Jester would regale him yet again until, at last, he ran through his entire repertoire of jokes, yet still the Sultan at sunset would go to the seashore and pray, "O Allah, send me my harem," so the Jester began to make funny hats out of tree-leaves and wore them as he behaved in all sorts of silly ways, and it amused and diverted the Sultan, until the next night, when he still went down to the seashore and prayed, "O Allah, send me my harem," until at length the Jester exhausted all the shtick he had at hand, so then he changed direction and began to tell the Sultan ghost stories, and that kept his attention for quite a while, though every day at sunset he still went down to the seashore and prayed, "O Allah, send me my harem," until at length the Jester ran out of ghost stories, so he began devising elaborate belabored stories with preposterous punch-lines, and when he could not think of any others, he threw himself into composing clever songs that he sang to the Sultan, who was always and ever amused until the following sunset when he still went down to the seashore and prayed, "O Allah, send me my harem," and at long last the poor Jester announced that he had no more funny songs to sing, or clever jests to tell, or spooky ghost stories to share, or anything whatever to pass the time and cheer up his master, so finally the Sultan was absolutely at his wit's end.

"Then," said Abe Grandbody, "it was finally the turn of the last of the three men who shared the penthouse on the forty-fifth floor, and he told his companions that he appreciated the efforts they'd made to pass the time as they climbed past the thirtieth floor, and he could not presume to surpass them singing funny songs or telling risible anecdota, so the only thing left for him was to tell a sad story for the remainder of their journey.

" 'And here's my story,' " he said. " 'There were once three men who lived in the penthouse of a forty-five-story building, and one day the elevator went on the fritz, so they decided to walk up the stairs, and to pass the time the first of them said he would sing them songs for the first fifteen floors, and indeed he did, after which the second of the three promised that he would tell amusing tales for the next fifteen floors, and he did that, too. And the last of the three said that he would pass the time it took to go up to the penthouse by relating a sad story, but he said he only had one to tell... '

At which point, the first of the three men said, 'Now just a moment! This sad story that you're starting to tell us sounds suspiciously like our own plight!'

" 'Indeed it is,' the third man agreed. 'The story is sad because just as we reached the thirtieth floor, I realized I'd locked the key to the front door of our apartment inside the penthouse... ' "

XXXViX

THE SHAGGY DOG LECTURE

"T he kind of jokes that I like best, you see, are of the so-called shaggy dog variety," Abe Grandbody continued. "The one about the three men living in the penthouse of a forty-five-story building is not strictly a shaggy dog tale— pun intended— though the one about the Sultan and his Jester is. Now there have been exceptions to my way of thinking, notably in a study of shaggy dog jokes by a humorist who wrote that the definition of the genre depends on the introduction of an element of fantasy, as well as what might be termed a "balloon-prick-deflation" ending.

"I disagree. Those qualities are often aspects of shaggy doggery, but there are other variables to the form, which I shall soon enumerate."

Here, a few of his captured, if not captivated auditors groaned.

Paying them no never-mind, to borrow a phrase from Walt Kelly, the former lifeguard continued his lecture. "There is but one characteristic that is inflexibly fixed, and that is that shaggy dog stories must be enormously long, for their chief aesthetic property must be to inflict a mammoth trial upon the patience of listeners, for it is, of course, primarily an auditory art form.[14]

---

[14] Thus readers may wonder what justification there can be for this book. Yr. Humble Piescribe salutes their perspicacity. Other readers may object to the term "art form." (Publisher's note: For the "auditory"experience, try the audiobook.)

"As for said length, it may be fashioned out of inordinate repetition, or it may, besides inordinate repetition, attain its size with a variety of colorful or/and fantastic incident, not to mention seemingly endless digression. The

exact mix generally depends upon the taste and artfulness —" (Here his audience provoked him with a round of snickers and guffaws.) "—I say, the taste and artfulness of the raconteur, for the form is improvisatory in nature."

Grandbody ticked off points on his fingers. "So we have the constant of great length, along with the variables of incident or/and repetition. All in all, the chief effect intended is to drive listeners to distraction, though it is also hoped that the process of whatever story is being told will simultaneously amuse the very same frustrated auditors. In short—" (Another raucous outburst here occurred.) "—we have a verbal anecdote that varies with each telling, culminating... pay attention! this is new!... with a punchline that will either be—

"1. Weak.

"2. A dreadful pun, which, of course, may also satisfy my first condition.

"3. The absolute worst sort is when there is no punchline at all.

"Now because I do not wish to bore you gentlemen..." (This produced so great an outburst of snarls, laughter, and regurgitation, the latter mostly pretended, that it was several minutes before the ex-lifeguard could end his sentence.)

"I will now complete my thought, which is that I shall give you examples of the first two sorts of shaggy dog story punchlines, but if you behave yourselves, I will omit the third and worst kind."

For once they all were silent.

XL

THE EXEMPLARY LECTURE OF ABRAHAM GRANDBODY

H e cleared his throat and drank some tea, taking care not to crunch the sugar cube in it between his teeth, lest he be mistaken for a peasant. "Now because you showed me some respect just now, I shall not exasperate your patience with an example of the third variety of joke, the kind without a punchline, for I was told such a tale once, which the speaker claimed was 'The original shaggy dog joke,' though I am certain it was not; it was, however, artless and, all in all, horrendous, so I shall not tell it to you.[15]

"Here, however, is an example of my second classification—and I shall mercifully tell it in truncated form." (That produced a few feeble expressions of gratitude.)

Ludovico Tschaperangeli was an orchestra conductor commissioned to lead the Greater Vacilian Musicale Chorale and Friday-Night Buswash Service in a performance of Beethoven's Symphony in D Minor, which requires a full chorus and soloists in its final movement. Unfortunately, the

---

[15] Grandbody doubtlessly referred to the story of the little boy who saw a shaggy dog one day in an alley and said to himself, "That is a shaggy dog, a very shaggy dog, an extremely shaggy dog," so he took it home, and his parents said, "That is a shaggy dog, a very shaggy dog, an extremely shaggy dog," and they allowed their son to keep the animal.

ruler of Vacilia decided to sing the bass part himself. His Uncertain Nibs (HUN), as his people called him, could never be relied to follow through on anything except to drain whichever bottle of booze he had in his hand. During orchestral rehearsals, HUN was always sneaking off to tipple and often missed his cue when he ought to have been warbling forth "Seid umschlungen." So the conductor hit upon a plan to ensure his bass soloist would be there on time, and it was to send off the tenor of the piece (Prince Tenorpiece) to the Royal Schnapsstop just as the third movement came to a close. The prince would then rouse HUN in time to stagger back to the concert hall and sing, "O, Freunde... ", et cetera.

Ludovico, however, was a bit absent-minded, so to remind himself to remind the prince to remind the king, he knotted a piece of string around his orchestral score at the page just before the fourth and final movement began, so that, on seeing the string, he could yank it off and point his baton at his tenor, who would then duly trot out to the neighboring pub and get the king who, though sloshed to the gillyflowers, yet managed to sozzle his way back to the concert stage and admonish the orchestra no longer to play "diese toene."

And therefore, on the evening of the great performance the audience could feel the tension for, as a journalist named W. Windchill Factor reported on the radio, "It's the bottom of the Ninth, the score is tied, and the bass is loaded."

---

15 (continued) So he decided to enter it into a local dog contest, and the first judge said, "That is a shaggy dog," and the second judge said, "That is a very shaggy dog," while the third judge said, "That is an extremely shaggy dog," and lo and behold, wonder of wonders, miracle of miracles, the dog won. So the boy decided to enter his pet in a city-wide dog contest and the first judge said, "That is a shaggy dog," and the second judge said, "That is a very shaggy dog," while the third

"But now," Abe Grandbody declared over the groans, "let us have a prime shaggy example of a punchline both weak and punnish. This story also shows the oral nature of the genre, for I am certain it would suffer if written down, as its climax is— how shall I put it?— onomatopoeic."

Here, W. Windchill Factor interrupted, "I do hope you don't intend to tell us that dreadful skooshmaker story?"

"Or the cushmaker?" Rudy Woods objected.

"Or the plopmaker!" grumbled a small European prisoner who had not spoken before.

"Or any other variation on that stupid story!" squeaked A. Q. Nameless.

"Not at all, not at all," Grandbody demurred. "I am about to tell you the tale of the rare ruby-hued, ancient Persian, wafer-thin, long-necked translucent Tysglas. Have any of you heard this one?"

The other prisoners put their heads together for a moment. "Unfortunately," W. W. Factor sighed, "we haven't."

---

15 (continued again) judge said, "That is an extremely shaggy dog," and lo and behold, wonder of wonders, miracle of miracles, the dog won. So the boy entered his pet in a state-wide dog contest and the first judge said, "That is a shaggy dog," and the second judge said, "That is a very shaggy dog," while the third judge said, "That is an extremely shaggy dog," and lo and behold, wonder of wonders, miracle of miracles, the dog won. So the boy entered his pet in a national dog contest and the first judge said, "That is a shaggy dog," and the second judge said, "That is a very shaggy dog," while the third judge said, "That is an extremely shaggy dog," and lo and behold, wonder of wonders, miracle of miracles, the dog won.

So the boy entered his pet in a hemispherical dog contest and the first judge said, "That is a shaggy dog," and the second judge said, "That is a very shaggy dog," while the third judge said, "That is an extremely shaggy dog," and lo and

Once upon a time there dwelt in Manhattan Lincoln Diogenes, a wealthy curator of a museum of curiosa and antiquities. Not only did he tend the museum's artifacts, he was himself an enthusiastic collector of priceless objets, with an especial interest in jugs, vases, and miscellaneous glassware.

His collection was displayed along with the museum's, as he derived much pleasure from showing off his personal prizes, and he frequently scheduled lecture-demonstrations that focused on the unique attributes of various pieces on display. He always held such events when he or the museum acquired some new archeological wonder. Now every true collector knows that there comes a time when every

---

15 (continued even more)   behold, wonder of wonders, miracle of miracles, the dog won. So the boy entered his pet in an international dog contest and the first judge said, "That is a shaggy dog," and the second judge said, "That is a very shaggy dog," while the third judge said, "That is an extremely shaggy dog," and lo and behold, wonder of wonders, miracle of miracles, the dog won.

So the boy entered his pet in a global dog contest and the first judge said, "That is a shaggy dog," and the second judge said, "That is a very shaggy dog, and lo and behold, wonder of wonders, miracle of miracles, the dog won. So the boy entered his pet in a dog contest and the first judge said, "That is a shaggy dog," and the second judge said, "That is a very shaggy dog," while the third judge said, "That is an extremely shaggy dog," and lo and behold, wonder of wonders, miracle of miracles, the dog won.

So the boy entered his pet in the Inner Solar System dog contest and the first judge said, "That is a shaggy dog," and the second judge said, "That is a very shaggy dog," while the third judge said, "That is an extremely shaggy dog," and lo and behold, wonder of wonders, miracle of miracles, the dog won. So the boy entered his pet in a Triplanetary dog contest and the first judge said, "That is a shaggy dog," and the

possible item on one's list is at long last acquired, but that happy occasion had not yet arrived for the museum curator, for there was one artifact that Diogenes had never been able to find, and without it, he knew he could not claim title to being the world's greatest collector of jugs, vases, and miscellaneous glassware.

---

15 (continued yet again)   second judge said, "That is a very shaggy dog," while the third judge (from Mars) said, "Yanqo du mi chylas yggla wvv," which, translated, means, "That is an extremely shaggy dog," and lo and behold, wonder of wonders, miracle of miracles, the dog won. So the boy entered his pet in the Grand Cosmic dog contest and the first judge, said, "Woof arf bark woof!" (He was from the Dog Star – no, Sirius-ly!), while the second judge said, "Thzzh vvy shggwy dk." (He was from earth, but he'd misplaced his dentures), and the third judge said, "Przyxlyrrrrrattt." (He was a stutterer). And lo and behold, wonder of wonders, miracle of miracles, the dog won.

So the boy entered his pet in a Megagalactic dog contest and the first judge communicated in sine language, which was rather angular, and the second judge said, "Chewbacca!" while the third judge said, "That is an extremely shaggy dog!" (He was a linguist.) And lo and behold, wonder of wonders, miracle of miracles, the dog won. So the boy entered his pet in the Augagalagapalaxian dog contest (Central System lingo for really big dog show) and the first judge, a military man, said, "Dog, shaggy," and the second judge, who was a revisionist, said, "Dog, hairy," while the third judge pedantically declared, "Caninensis, hirsuitus," and lo and behold, wonder of wonders, miracle of miracles, the dog won.

Now the boy thought that his pet had won every possible honor imaginable, but to his surprise, he soon received an invitation to enter his dog into the Greater Paratemporal Dog Contest, and the boy did, so the first judge said, "That used to be shaggy dog," and the second judge said, "That is a very shaggy dog," while the third judge said, "That

15 (yes, still continued yet again) will be an extremely shaggy dog!"
And lo and behold, wonder of wonders, miracle of miracles,
the dog won, did win, and will win.

"OK," the boy thought, "now that is indeed it! There
cannot possibly be any more dog contests." So he decided the
next thing he ought to do would be think of a name for his dog.
But to his great surprise, he suddenly received an invitation to
enter his pet in the Agglomerated Nirvanistic Paralleladog
Contest, and the boy did, so the first judge said, "In respect to
dog, shaggy," and the second judge was about to say,
"Shaggy, indeed, greatly achieved," but the third judge
shouted, "No dogs allowed!" But in spite of the dispute that
followed, lo and behold, wonder of wonders, miracle of
miracles, the dog won. By now, an entire year had passed, so,
to maintain his pet's standing, the boy reentered his dog in his
local dog contest, and the first judge said, "That is a shaggy
dog!" and the second judge said, "That is a very shaggy dog!"
while the third judge said, "That is an extremely shaggy dog!"
and lo and behold, wonder of wonders, miracle of miracles, the
dog won.

So the boy reentered the dog in the city-wide dog
contest, and the first judge said, "That is a shaggy dog!" and
the second judge said, "That is a very shaggy dog!" while the
third judge said, "That is an extremely shaggy dog!" and lo and
behold, wonder of wonders, miracle of miracles, the dog won.
So the boy reentered the dog in the county-wide dog contest
and the first judge said, "That is a shaggy dog!" and the second
judge said, "That is a very shaggy dog!" while the third judge
said, "That is an extremely shaggy dog!" and lo and behold,
wonder of wonders, miracle of miracles, the dog won. So the
boy reentered the dog in the state-wide dog contest and the
first judge said, "That is a shaggy dog!" and the second judge
said, "That is a very shaggy dog!" while the third judge said,
"That is an extremely shaggy dog!" and lo and behold, wonder
of wonders, miracle of miracles, the dog won.

So the boy reentered the dog in the national dog
contest and the first judge said, "That is a shaggy dog!" and the
second judge said, "That is a very shaggy dog!" while the third
judge said, "That is an extremely shaggy dog!" and lo and

---

15 (continued, can you believe it?)   behold, wonder of wonders, miracle of miracles, the dog won. So the boy reentered the dog in the hemispherical dog contest and the first judge said, "That is a shaggy dog!" and the second judge said, "That is a very shaggy dog!" while the third judge said, "That is an extremely shaggy dog!" and lo and behold, wonder of wonders, miracle of miracles, the dog won.

So the boy reentered the dog in the international dog contest and the first judge said, "That is a shaggy dog!" and the second judge said, "That is a very shaggy dog!" while the third judge said, "That is an extremely shaggy dog!" and lo and behold, wonder of wonders, miracle of miracles, the dog won. So the boy reentered the dog in the global dog contest and the first judge said, "That is a shaggy dog!" and the second judge said, "That is a very shaggy dog!" while the third judge said, "That is an extremely shaggy dog!" and lo and behold, wonder of wonders, miracle of miracles, the dog won.

So the boy reentered the dog in the Inner Solar System dog contest and the first judge said, "That is a shaggy dog!" and the second judge said, "That is a very shaggy dog!" while the third judge said, "That is an extremely shaggy dog!" and lo and behold, wonder of wonders, miracle of miracles, the dog won. So the boy reentered the dog in the Triplanetary dog contest and the first judge said, "That is a shaggy dog!" and the second judge said, "That is a very shaggy dog!" while the third judge said, "That is an extremely shaggy dog!" (because, by now, due to a revival of right-wing Republicanism, English had been declared the official language of the known universe) and lo and behold, wonder of wonders, miracle of miracles, the dog won. So the boy reentered the dog in the Grand Cosmic dog contest and the first judge said, "That is a shaggy dog!" and the second judge said, "That is a very shaggy dog!" while the third judge said, "That is an extremely shaggy dog!" and lo and behold, wonder of wonders, miracle of miracles, the dog won.

So the boy reentered the dog in the Megagalactic dog contest and the first judge said, "That is a shaggy dog!" and the second judge said, "That is a very shaggy dog!" while the third judge said, "That is an extremely shaggy dog!" and lo and behold, wonder of wonders, miracle of miracles, the dog won.

---

15 (continued—you've got to be kidding!)[16]   So the boy reentered the dog in the Augagalagapalaxian dog contest and the first judge said, "That is a shaggy dog!" and the second judge said, "That is a very shaggy dog!" while the third judge said, "That is an extremely shaggy dog!" and lo and behold, wonder of wonders, miracle of miracles, the dog won. So the boy reentered the dog in the   Greater Paratemporal dog contest and the first judge said, "That was a shaggy dog!" and the second judge said, "That is a very shaggy dog!" while the third judge said, "That will be an extremely shaggy dog!" and lo and behold, wonder of wonders, miracle of miracles, the dog did win, won, and will win.

So the boy reentered the dog in the Agglomerated Nirvanistic Paralleldog contest and the first judge said, "Dogs have been known to be shaggy!" and the second judge said, "Shagginess must be carried to great lengths!" while the third judge said, "An extremely shaggy dog is like a deep well!" which produced a serious argument between the judges that took many years to resolve (he admitted it was only true sometimes), but lo and behold, wonder of wonders, miracle of miracles, the dog won. And now the boy was certain that his dog was the shaggiest and therefore best in the universe and elsewhere, then, now and to-be, and it was certainly to think of a name for the mutt. But to his great surprise, he received an invitation to enter his pet in the Incomprehensative Universanononistical Lobachevskian dog contest, in which, it was declared, the TOP DOG would be selected from all times and all places and everywhere there was, is, and will be forever and ever, Amen! So the boy said to himself, "Hoo-boy! Now this one is Really BIG TIME!"

So, of course, he knew he had to enter his pet in the Incomprehensative Universanononistical Lobachevskian dog contest, and as they have been known to declare in Yorkshire, eigh, by gum, he did! So he bought new clothes for himself (all the competitions he'd won brought in some big bucks!) and he

---

[16] PUBLISHER'S NOTE: This may be the longest footnote in history, although don't quote us since we have nothing to back that up. But, yee gads! You'd think, right?

The single item that was missing was a rare ruby-hued, ancient Persian, wafer-thin, long-necked translucent Tysglas.

(It should be noted that Grandbody pronounced each word very slowly, for he was a member of the S. T. O. A. For details, consult the audio cassette Bob and Ray, the Two and Only, still available from amazon.com.)

It is customary at this point for the raconteur to take a dramatic pause as if he or she is about to get to the point of the story. When, however, the tale-teller's hiatus goes on and on and on, it is likely— and expected— for the auditor(s) to break the silence by saying something like, "Well? What happened next?" It is then mandatory for the raconteur to turn her or his attention to the questioner(s) and reply, "I'm not

---

15 (continued—how long can this persist?)   got his dog a brand-new collar, and they went off to the Incomprehensative Universanononistical Lobachevskian dog contest, where no Republicans were allowed, so the gwylp mogfozzer derf, "KaBLAH kaBLAH!," and the plywg fogmozzer derf, "KAblah KAblah!" while the phywylmyl schylmystyr, who was half-Welsh, glimmelarped, "Ilygwhyly amawha pyngltyllangellal ryfflly!" and lo and behold, wonder of wonders, miracle of miracles, the dog won. So to summarize, the boy's dog's history, for two years he had entered local, city-wide, county-wide, state-wide, national, hemispherical, international, global, inner solar system, triplanetary, grand cosmic, megagalactic, augagalagapalaxian, paratemporal, and agglomerated nirvanistic parallelodog contests, and at each the first judges said, "This is a shaggy dog!" and the second judges said, "This is a very shaggy dog!" while the third judges said, "This is an extremely shaggy dog!" and lo and behold, wonder of wonders, miracle of miracles, the dog won each and every contest, not to mention also coming in TOP DOG at the Incomprehensative Universanononistical Lobachevskian dog contest, where no Republicans are allowed. Now is all of this clear, or do you

sure what In the whole world, there were only three remaining ruby-hued, ancient Persian, wafer-thin, long-necked translucent Tysglasses, hence their rarity. One belonged to Grimsley Woax, a British collector. The second was the property of Cholly Frexelpath, exiled governor of Usui, and the third rare ruby-hued, ancient Persian, wafer-thin, long-necked translucent Tysglas had recently been stolen, along with other curios, from the home of J. Pierpont Kotzwinkle, who made his fortune in polyunsaturated flax.

Diogenes decided to write to Grimsley Woax to see whether he would consider selling him his rare ruby-hued, ancient Persian, wafer-thin, long-necked translucent Tysglas. Soon Diogenes received a letter from England which said, "Yes, I will gladly sell you my rare ruby-hued, ancient Persian, wafer-thin, long-necked translucent Tysglas. The price is one million pounds sterling, plus thirty cases of Pat's cheesesteaks with the works."

It was a steep price, but it was met, and thanks to the internet, Diogenes did not even have to go to Philadelphia for the sandwiches. His savings, of course, were now quite compromised, but it was worth it to be able to declare himself the world's preeminent collector of jugs, vases, and miscellaneous glassware. Arrangements were made for the

---

15 (continued—last one, promise) wish it to be repeated in entirety, or in part? Are you certain? Very well, then... you're asking me. Could you explain?" This will quite likely elicit a more forceful repetition of the question— "What happens next?" This, of course, is the moment that the incurable shaggy dogster has been waiting for. He or she now will affix his audience with a thoroughly perplexed look, such as one might bestow upon an especially dim-witted child, and say, "What on earth do you mean, 'What happened next?' Haven't you been following what I said? Should I summarize it again for you?" Naturally the tormented auditors will vigorously negate that notion.

rare ruby-hued, ancient Persian, wafer-thin, long-necked translucent Tysglas to be flown to Kennedy Airport, and the curator went there and

waited anxiously till the plane arrived. But just as it taxied onto the runway, one of its landing-wheels skittered slightly over a pebble and when his crate was at last removed, he was dismayed to discover that the plane's slight impact had shattered his rare ruby-hued, ancient Persian, wafer-thin, long-necked translucent Tysglas.

After a period of sheer grief, Diogenes set out to track down Cholly Frexelpath, whom he traced to New Jersey, where he was enjoying political asylum at a tavern owned by Tony Soprano.

The curator asked Frexelpath whether he would consider selling him his rare ruby-hued, ancient Persian, wafer-thin, long-necked translucent Tysglas. Cholly replied, "I heard about your bad luck with the first one you bought, so, tell you what, I'm going to let you have mine as a donation to your museum."

"That," Lincoln Diogenes happily declared, "is a generous offer!"

"But there's a catch," Frexelpath warned him. "It's in storage in Zanzibar. You'll have to pay the warehouse costs and have it delivered."

"Gladly!" the curator declared. "After all, how much can that be?"

"Last time they billed me," Cholly replied, "it was a little over a hundred thousand dollars."

---

15 (continued—one more. We lied) The dogster will now say something like, "Then I've got a question. The dog has won all conceivable and inconceivable dog contests in every possible space-time referent. What else could happen?"
(Exit— at once!)

Diogenes blanched. His funds were certainly dwindling... but the thought of finally owning a rare ruby-hued, ancient Persian, wafer-thin, long-necked translucent Tysglas was too heady to resist, so he paid off the warehouse and this time, not trusting airplanes, decided to have his rare ruby-hued, ancient Persian, wafer-thin, long-necked translucent Tysglas shipped to New York harbor.

One afternoon in late spring he stood on a dock on the Hudson River and eagerly waited for the ship to arrive and bring him his rare ruby-hued, ancient Persian, wafer-thin, long-necked translucent Tysglas.

But just as the vessel was being tied to the dock, it bumped against a piling. Upon opening up the packing crate, poor Diogenes was crushed to find the rare ruby-hued, ancient Persian, wafer-thin, long-necked translucent Tysglas in the same condition as he was. Well, of course, the curator was inconsolable. He'd squandered his fortune on a dream that lay in pieces— not once, but twice!— and he still did not own a rare ruby-hued, ancient Persian, wafer-thin, long-necked translucent Tysglas.

There was no point in getting in touch with J. Pierpont Kotzwinkle. His rare ruby-hued, ancient Persian, wafer-thin, long-necked translucent Tysglas, you may recall, had been stolen.

One day, Lincoln Diogenes disconsolately wandered into a dusty second-hand curio shop, not that he could afford to buy much of anything. But lo and behold, wonder of wonders, miracle of miracles, what did he discover in a dimly-lit recess, perched precariously on the edge of a table, but a rare ruby-hued, ancient Persian, wafer-thin, long-necked translucent Tysglas!

No, he thought, this is not A rare ruby-hued, ancient Persian, wafer-thin, long-necked translucent Tysglas— there is only one left in the world, so this must be THE rare ruby-hued, ancient Persian, wafer-thin, long-necked translucent Tysglas!

He sought out the shopkeeper and said in an offhanded manner, "So how much do you want for this piece of crap?"

"Buck," that worthy replied.

The curator gleefully paid it and took it to the museum, walking all the way, even though it was a distance of well over three miles. Lovingly cuddling his prize, he carefully washed his rare ruby-hued, ancient Persian, wafer-thin, long-necked translucent Tysglas till it shined and sparkled.

But then an awful thought suddenly occurred to him. His newly-acquired rare ruby-hued, ancient Persian, wafer-thin, long-necked translucent Tysglas was, after all, stolen! It did not truly belong to him, it was the property of J. Pierpont Kotzwinkle, the flax millionaire.

Now if Lincoln Diogenes had been solely a private collector, he might have considered keeping his rare ruby-hued, ancient Persian, wafer-thin, long-necked translucent Tysglas a secret, but he was, after all, a respected museum curator, and he had a public trust to consider. Not to return the rare ruby-hued, ancient Persian, wafer-thin, long-necked translucent Tysglas to J. Pierpont Kotzwinkle would be, in effect, to condone theft, and if he did that, he would be, at least in his own mind and heart, inviting robbers to pillage his own beloved antiquarian collection and museum artifacts. Besides which, he had every intention of displaying his rare ruby-hued, ancient Persian, wafer-thin, long-necked translucent Tysglas to the public, but that would be tantamount to announcing himself as the receiver of stolen goods.

No, there was no choice but to get in touch with J. Pierpont Kotzwinkle and inform him that he had found the rare ruby-hued, ancient Persian, wafer-thin, long-necked translucent Tysglas in a second-hand curio shop. But to the curator's amazement and delight, the flax millionaire called him on the phone and said, "I got your message about my stolen rare ruby-hued, ancient Persian, wafer-thin, long-necked translucent Tysglas. Look, as far as I'm concerned you can keep that dust-catcher!"

Diogenes was amazed. "But it's the only one in the world!"

"That's right," J. Pierpont Kotzwinkle agreed. "The insurance company paid me a lot of money for it, and I don't want it turning up again."

"But I was going to display it at my museum!"

Kotzwinkle soothed him. "No reason you can't. Everyone has heard of your hard luck with those other two rare ruby-hued, ancient Persian, rare ruby-hued, ancient Persian, wafer-thin, long-necked translucent Tysglasses. We've all felt bad for you, but look, you're an internationally respected antiquarian— so just announce you've found a unique variant of the rare ruby-hued, ancient, wafer-thin, long-necked translucent Tysglas. Call it, instead, a rare ruby-hued, ancient Sumerian, wafer-thin, long-necked translucent Tysbotl, and we'll both be happy."

"A brilliant idea! Thank you!" Diogenes declared, ringing off.

Soon after that, the curator made his announcement to the press, and as Kotzwinkle had predicted, he was showered with messages of congratulations that at last he was the world's leading expert collector of jugs, vases, and miscellaneous glassware.

He sent invitations to art critics, archeologists, collectors, educators, and the press to come and see his rare ruby-hued, ancient Sumerian, wafer-thin, long-necked translucent Tysbotl, and, as they say (or rather sing), "Paragraphs got into all the papers."

The great day arrived. Guests eagerly thronged the museum's great lecture hall. Upon a platform at the front of the room was a plain, unornamented table on which rested six colorful glass flasks in a row.

Lincoln Diogenes greeted everyone and proceeded to tell them a slightly revised version of his adventures as he attempted to secure a rare ruby-hued, ancient Persian, wafer-thin, long-necked translucent Tysglas, and how, after losing two of them, enjoyed the serendipitous pleasure of finding, instead, a rare ruby-hued, ancient Sumerian, wafer-thin, long-necked translucent Tysbotl, which was almost as good!

"This is it," he said, pointing to the fourth one from the right (stage right) on the table. "And now," he said, stepping behind the row of bottles and flasks, "allow me to demonstrate the unique properties of the rare ruby-hued, ancient Sumerian, wafer-thin, long-necked translucent Tysbotl."

Beginning with the end of the row, stage right, he tapped each flask with a rubber mallet. The audience heard tones equivalent to— "My coun-try tys of thee."

With that, Abe Grandbody sat down swiftly, for W. Windchill Factor had just tapped him with a rubber mallet. "Which proves," he declared, "that he is literally a numbskull."

XLI

A NAMELESS REPRISE

The next day, Rudy Woods turned to A. Q. Nameless. "We haven't heard from you yet."

Now do recall: this book is a reconstruction of the Siberian Peach Pie story I wrote to Daniel Pinkwater. Most of the current chapter was sent as one side of a thirty-minute audio cassette. Though impossible to reproduce here in that form, what follows is a fairly accurate transcription, originally rendered in as squeaky a voice as possible.

"Once upon a time, there was this vacuum cleaner salesman, and he went to Siberia because he was a new employee, and that's where his company always starts its men. He was a very good salesman and sold out all his stock.

"Just before he caught the return ship to California, where he meant to get more vacuum cleaners, he got hungry. He saw all these Cossacks riding along yelling, "Hail to the Czar! Down with the Bolsheviks!" Then the salesman saw this sign: Siberian Restaurant. Cooler inside." So he went in and had a meal, and at the end, he asked what they had for dessert, and the manager said, "Siberian Peach Pie."

The salesman ordered a slice. He discovered Siberian Peach Pie is the most delicious, scrumptious, sensationally mysterious appealing dessert upon the earth! He gobbled it down and ordered another piece.

The manager shook his head. "Sorry, but that's the last I've got. The factory will send us some when we order more."

The salesman did not have time to wait since his ship was about to sail, so he resolved to sail back to America, get some more vacuum cleaners, and return as fast as possible for another slice of Siberian Peach Pie. Which he did… but on the return trip, the ship hit an iceberg and the vessel sank. The vacuum cleaner salesman survived. Floating in the sea, clinging to a piece of driftwood, he mumbled to himself, "Siberian Peach Pie, Siberian Peach Pie, Siberian Peach Pie."

W. Windchill Factor nudged the speaker, so he went on with his story.

"Now the ocean currents are very strange. They cast him on the strange Isle of— I don't know what it's called, but it's a frozen northern island. The natives found him half-dead and decided to finish the job. But the tribe did not realize that their prey was awake and he managed to escape, or almost. A big wall of ice stopped him. He dug into it furiously with both hands, but just before he broke through one of the natives ran up with a big machete and lopped off one of his arms. He broke through the ice, and fell into the ocean. Fortunately, it was so cold that the icy water immediately cauterized the wound. But the shock was so bad that he went into a coma and drifted and drifted and drifted, mumbling to himself, "Siberian Peach Pie, Siberian Peach Pie, Siberian Peach Pie…"

Factor again had to prod him to get him unstuck.

"Now the ocean currents, as I think I said, are strange," the Nameless narrator went on, "and eventually they cast him onto the beach of San Francisco… "

At this point in the original audio cassette, there was an eighteen-minute gap, presumably the fault of a secretary who used to work in Washington.

" 'Hail, Stalin! Down with Capitalists! HEY! You there, you with the Ping Pong ball head, that's not allowed! You must be a spy! You're under arrest!' "

"And so they threw him in jail. And here I am."

This concludes the oral transcription.

– Yr. Humble Piescribe

When the Nameless prisoner sat down, the two inmates who had not yet told their tales regarded him very strangely.

"What's the matter?" he squeaked at them. "Don't you believe me?"

"It's not that," said the smaller of the two, a man lacking a left arm. "It's just that the two of us have a lot in common!"

"We do?" A. Q. Nameless turned to the last inmate, a gentleman with the air of someone both European and affluent. "And does that go for you, too?"

"In some ways, yes." His tone was cultivated and cultured. "In some ways, not at all."

That caught everyone's attention.

XLii

THEME, WiTH VARiATiONS

The one-armed man clutched a woolen blanket, for he was shivering. He introduced himself as Quincy Aloysius Nonamis and told his cellmates that, "for various reasons, my adventures also brought me here to Russia, where I, too, have experienced the wonders of Siberian Peach Pie. But it happened to me in an altogether different fashion. I got lost in the snow one day, and, seeing a farm in the distance, went there and begged the farmer to be allowed to come inside to get warm. He was a kindly fellow, so not only did he take me into his house, but his wife served me a splendid meal, culminating in just the dessert you know I'm going to state. Well, I was so impressed with Siberian Peach Pie that I begged the lady for the recipe, and she was pleased to oblige me."

"She did?!" our Nameless hero exclaimed, hopping up and down in feverish excitement. "You actually have the recipe?"

"Yes," the speaker nodded, "but that alone is not enough, for the farmer's wife explained that the pie must be made with only one kind of peach, and they cannot be found anywhere but Siberia. Fortunately, though, the farmer had an orchard of Siberian peach trees, and was good enough to provide me with a large quantity of pits, so in a short time I planted my own peach orchard."

"You, sir, are a truly great man!" A. Q. Nameless proclaimed.

A Nonamis sigh. "That's good of you to say so, but as I was about to enjoy my first harvest, my orchard suffered a sudden attack of Siberian peach fly, which ruined my entire crop and killed the trees as well."

"Bad luck," Rudy Woods said. "What did you do then?"

"I went around killing every Siberian peach fly I could find... not knowing that it is a protected Russian species. So that's how I landed in jail with all of you. But at least my sentence is almost over. In a few days," Q. A. declared, "I'll return to that farm and try to get some more peach pits and start all over again."

"Such a sad story," said our Nameless hero. "I feel like giving you a hug."

Beneath his breath, W. Windchill Factor muttered, "That I'd like to see."

XLiii

THE FINAL SPEAKER

The cultured European gentleman rose. "My name is John Stone," he said.

What a strange name, all the other prisoners thought.

Fishing through his pockets, Stone withdrew a sheaf of crumpled papers written upon in a clear, elegant hand. "I have been in this prison quite a bit longer than the rest of you. Because I've been here so long, to pass the weary time I have written down my story, though I admit I have indulged myself here and there with flights of parodistic fancy."

"What's that mean?" Rudy Woods blurted.

"You'll see," said Stone, then gave Rudy an appraising glance. "Perhaps you won't. But if none of you object, I shall read what I've written."

Except for an occasional snore, no one objected, so John Stone opened his manuscript and started to read.

XLIV

INTERRAMBLE — RE JOYCE!

Stone waved a hand at Nameless and Nonamis and began.

"Funny be that thee and me have kinlike unkined unkinned shinned unskinned interactivity, but I improvise in style. Here's my story as written...

"By my round eye I espy like an arch starched and rounded (gonggonggong) to wit, a verismanaceous tailtalltale.

"O once I was a little kiddle.
Mama called me 'liddle piddle.'
She said, said she, 'Hello, hi!
Come and eat delicious pie!'
"Three, four, and what is more,
all my eye delights in pi.

"Crustily, crustily, in the bowl by the basin shining replete with the fierce pride of place that rallied stern Stern, renegade hero of Whissinschussel, the capital of my land, where I would teach preach reach with all the tangled angles down below the town the tin the tan the plan Ed McMahon, all of this, you see, I call they call all call one and all! BAVARIA! At Mama's pippippip I slip the plate my pate and ate and ate and ate! But I state it might be too late!"

XLV

THE BAVARIAN CREAM PIE STORY

O nce upon a time," the prisoner read, "a youth named John Stone lived in the small town of Wyblgt, which is easy to spell, but difficult to pronounce. He was the son of Ebeazezer Murgatroyd Stone, which is easy to pronounce, but difficult to spell, and his Mama, Ruth Meggasniffles. The finest thing in his life, Stone thought, always was and is his Mama's magnificent Bavarian Cream Pie, so named because Wyblgt is nestled in the Bavarian mountains."

"Does Bavaria have mountains?" W. Windchill Factor interrupted.

"Yes, the Bavarian Alps," Stone replied, "and thank you for staying awake. Now every day when I came from school, Mama would set before me her most freshly-baked Bavarian Cream Pie. The secret of its excellence is an old family recipe handed down by her mother from her grandmother from her mother from her mother's mother, from her father, who liked to bake in the closet.

"Now I still have in my possession my Mama's secret recipe set down in her own admittedly atrocious misspelled handwriting. Shall I read it to you?"

The replies consisted of a chorus of snores, a long-suffering journalistic yawn, and a shoulder shrug from old Amos, who said, "Aww, what the hell— y' talked me into it."

XLVi

THE BAVARIAN CREAM PiE RECiPE

(by Ruth Meggasniffles)

Croost
Hull glomp mooshy flower
Creem
Big glatch hevvy stiff-womped creem

Flayfurings	Chock o' layte
Ape reekotta	Kah vah
Gallic	Tung
Kwinz	Koko not
A kwa veet	Quasha
Goosebelly	Usky back
Rock-hot la comb	Crammed belly
A voe cad'o	Limbubble
Go rape	Van or d'nair
Strawbubbly	Dingle belly
Bah na-na	Macarooni
Heh there	Whiled Torkee
Tee hee	Elton belly
Bier	Nestle roads
Hecklebelly	Xereth
Tsallam me	Fa-la or num
Blew belly	Ochs tayl
Eye rich	Yeahm
Tsliver vitch	Golly toby rack u
Cow daddos	Prosh & T no
John Quill	Zoo kee nee
Tummy may toe	

Bump frum on taybell croost.. Sit on it lots! Mayk hull boonch strips,—thurdee sicks.

Now tek hull bunch balls. Poot flayfurings in balls. Porsa linn balls is goodest. Should be for tee too. Tek big py ditch. Poot flayfurings on in layrs.

Top uff layrs poot croost – like sew: siv and teen strips wun wey oop-don. – niy and tinstrips bak-foorth udder wey.

Now bayk.

Shlep too taybell. Kut.

Noo? I shoodeet it, two?

XLVII

A STONY ULTIMATUM

N ow as the years passed, young John Stone grew to manhood, but every day of every year, he would feast upon another of his mother's superbly delicious Bavarian Cream Pies—

"Surprising you don't weigh five hundred pounds," W. Windchill Factor softly snarked.

"I work out a lot," Stone growled. "But I digress... On his eighteenth birthday, his father Ebeazezer said to his son, 'It is high time that you went out into the world to seek your fortune.'

"The youth accepted the ultimatum with a glad heart, for he was eager to see the world, so he made plans for his departure. On the morrow, he was ready to go. His Mama came to him and presented him with a large box that held twelve Bavarian Cream Pies, each with crusts of seventeen horizontal strips and nineteen vertical strips, also forty-two individual layers of cream, each with its own subtly different taste."[17]

---

[17] See preceding chapter

XLViii

MUCH ADiEU ABOUT CRUSTiNG

ACT I, Scene 1

The Bavarian Alps.

(Enter JOHN STONE, lugging a big box, a knapsack of clothes on his shoulder.)

JOHN

O'er this hilly climb full sore
For twenty hours, or maybe more
I've mounted high, descended low,
But still no town or place to go.
I'll sit me down, it's time to eat.
A slice of pie, that will be sweet.
I'll open up this great big box;
I need some pie, some beer, some lox.

(He eatteth the first of the twelve Bavarian Cream Pies.)

O exquisite B. C. pie!
You are a wonder to the eye
So filled with berries, booze and nuts
You are a pleasure to my guts!
But now I've et, I'd better slide
Right down this snowy mountainside.
To get to town, it sure will be
A shortcut, and it's also free!
Now grab the box, and poise the toe,
And hold the nose, and here I goooooooo—

ACT I, Scene 2.
A Swiss Hospital.

(JOHN STONE is in bed, his limbs merrily slung aloft. A NURSE enters.)

NURSE

Tomorrow, says the Doc, you'll mend,
And you may therefore elsewhere wend,
But not until you pay your bill.

JOHN STONE

But I have little in my purse. To fill
Its depths I ventured forth to find some work
But then I broke my legs.

NURSE

You jerk!
If you don't pay, we'll put them back the way they were,
And boot you out the door, you cur!

JOHN STONE

The only treasure I have here
Are Mama's pies, that's all, I fear.

NURSE

Well, if they're any good, who knows?
The Doc might take them, I suppose.

ACT II.

In Front of the Hospital.

(Enter JOHN STONE, carrying a much smaller box.
JOHN STONE)

JOHN

O woe is me, this sucks! I'm done!
My pies! They only left me one!
Should I go home and ask for more?
I think my Dad would get real sore.
A different plan I must devise
To stretch this pie. Now I surmise
That if I cut it carefully
And do not make a pig of me
A slice might even last a week.
And in that time, a job I'll seek!

(He cutteth the pie into twelve thin slices, packs them up, and
exits.)

XLIX

THE FIRST SLICE

And John Stone came unto a great city, and yea, as he walked its avenues and byways, he beheld a glittering panoply of commerce, of beautiful women riding in open carriages, cobblers and tinkers and tinklers and tailors and bakers and fakers and fakirs and bakirs, also much soldiery, bankfodder, and grandmommies.

And as he walked, and witnesseth the fruit of the world's womb, he said to himself, "I hath not seen aught to fellow this spectacle, and if I say not the sooth, I would befoul my pie with leeks!" (Elsewhere known as "taking a leek.")

So in this wondrous swirlpool, he sought for some way to make a living, but no employer showed any interest whatever until on the ninth day before Latke Eve, a swarthy sailor sidled up to him and saith, "One word of mine, and thine fortune shall be assured, but before I utter a syllable, first I crave THE FIRST SLICE of that exquisite pastry I see inside the box you carry."

So with much trepidation, Our Nameful Hero made the trade. Eftsoons[18] he sailed with his eleven remaining pie slices unto Ye New Worlde wherein, with further trepidation, he traded ten more of them for a noble span that arches over the lower reaches of elden Manahatta to forestland as yet unnamed.[19]

---

[18] Word employed with thanks to S. T. Coleridge.

[19] This, of course, is wholly anachronistic, but at this stage of the story, do you actually insist upon logic?

L

IS THAT A FAULKT?

i   Cause if it ain't complicated up enough, it ain't good enough for him, but what do you expect from a Bavarian? 'stead o' writin' home for more, or maybe even asking for the recipe, now that he only has a few slices left, and never mind how some folks'd call it an obsession, but anyhow so he sees it's bad but does he write home? Uh-uh, like I say, he's gotta complicate it up.

ii   But you have to understand, I talked it over with the sailor, who became my friend, who sold me the Brooklyn Bridge, who said, "Why not ask for the recipe? I can sell Bavarian Cream Pies, and give you five percent royalty, and you'll make even bigger bucks!"

Now that's a friend! But there was no way I could tell him Mama can't write, she can't hardly read, yet I did write her, but you could stand on your head and not figure out her recipe, so what I had to do, instead, now I was a rich bridge owner, was to go home and watch carefully while she made a pie so I could work out how she did it.

iii   Does he ask me for advice? No, he goes to Bavaria, so what happens next?

iv   Off coast. Up sails barbarians, more. Broadsides galore, but Cap'n has drowned cabin-boy in the Lowlands, so what can you expect from coarse Corsairs? Orphan! I hear this works, but no ice it cuts, such is myth, yet they make me deal:

my life, OK, but no pie, no bridge, they also throw recipe overboard!

v   Would you believe, Barbary pirates?! So now foreigners own Brooklyn Bridge, plus he's broke without any pie to his name!

Li

A FAREWELL TO HARMS

He is stopped. Four months, but he don't do a thing. Nothing. Nada. Nil. You can't fight it when it snows. Not a big snow. Not an avalanche. So he is stopped. Nada. No-no. Zilch. STOPPED.

Four months later.

Hard to drag all that way. When it's a mountain you've got to face, you've got to face it. Are you a man? Then you've got to face it. If you don't, you're not. Simple as that.

So what are you?

What he is is a man who drags. Bloody, but unbowed. A mentsch in a trench.

They find him.

They carry him home. Over the threshhold.

His Mama gives him a big hug, but he does not cry.

He is a man.

Lii

WAY TOO WEIRD FOR A TITLE

O, Mama, yes, I'm skin and bones.
They sent me up in the Big Ship, a Butte,
But I'm back, see? So now if you want to keep me
From cashing in my chips, Mama,
Bake me, please, a brand-new pie,
Bavarian, you know, with cream, and all:
With crust that's got seventeen— Count 'em!— strips
The ones that run back and forth, that's horizontal,
And nineteen more that run the other way,
The way that's vertical,
And under the crust, O Ma, O Ma!
Put forty-two— Count 'em!— slabs of cream,
And each and every one a subtly different taste—

(To the tune of "A Modern Major-General")

There's Ape reekotta, A kwa veet, Bah na-na and Blewbelly,

There's Avoe cad'o, Cow daddos, Rock-hot la comb and Goosebelly,

There's Chock o'layte and Koko not and Quasha, Kwinz and also Bier,

And Nestle roads and Usky back, and don't forget the Heh-eh there,

And Hecklebelly, Dingle belly, Macarooni, Limbubble,

Elton belly, Zoo kee nee, Fa-la or num,   on the double!

And don't leave out the Tsliver vitch, the Xereth or the Whiled Torkee.

They go so well with kendied Yeahm, washed down with pots of hot Tee hee.

THE FAMILY

They go so well (Etc.)

JOHN STONE

There's Golly toby rack u, Gallic, Tung, Ochs tayl, and Strawbubbly,

And Eye rich, Prosh & T no, Tsallah me and also Crammed belly,

There's Kah vah, Tummy may toe and John Quill, tasting very fair,

But don't leave out the Go Rape, and lots and lots Van or d'nair!

MAMA

I wish I could, my sonneleh, bake up a great big pie for thee,

But after you got lost at sea, I lost the stupid recipe!

With that, John Stone folded up his manuscript, put it back in his pocket, and sat down. He shrugged. "So you know what I told my Mama?"

"No, what?" the other prisoners (the ones still awake) asked.

He told them. It made a great impression both upon Q. A. Nonamis and our Nameless hero.

LIII

THE BEGINNING OF THE END

So it came to pass that A. Q. Nameless served his sentence in the Siberian prison, and the authorities planned to release him in one hour. So these are the generations of his final moments: sixty minutes, yet when he looked again, only fifty-nine of them remained, and like an hourglass, wherein doth run all the days of our lives, or like the lyricized bottles of malted brew on the wall, there were just fifty-eight minutes remaining, and then there were fifty-seven, which descended to fifty-six, which declined to fifty-five, which gave way to fifty-four, which stepped aside for fifty-three, which yielded place to fifty-two, which yielded to fifty-one, which acknowledged the legitimacy of mighty fifty, from which sprang a line of kin, to wit: forty-nine and forty-eight and forty-seven, forty-six and forty-five, those look-alikes forty-four and forty-three, forty-two and forty-one, and least of that clan, forty, which gave up the ghost to thirty-nine, thirty-eight, thirty-seven, thirty-six, thirty-five, thirty-four, thirty-three, thirty-two, thirty-one and then came thirty, holding position till it could be supplanted by twenty-nine, twenty-eight, twenty-seven, twenty-six, twenty-five, twenty-four, twenty-three, twenty-two, twenty-one and twenty, which was scattered by the energetic teens until at length he had a mere twelve minutes more of his sentence to go, and then only eleven, which chose ten, instead, then short-lived nine and eight and seven and six and five and four, three, two, and now he had but one minute more before he was free!

LIV

COUNTDOWN

And these are the generations of our Nameless hero's final minute: he saw there were but sixty seconds to go, and when he looked again only fifty-nine of them remained, and like a minute hand, whereon doth tick all the instants of our lives, or like the lyricized bottles of malted brew on the wall, there were just fifty-eight seconds remaining, and then there were but fifty-seven, which descended to fifty-six, which declined to fifty-five, which gave way to fifty-four, which stepped aside for fifty-three, which yielded place to fifty-two, which yielded to fifty-one, which acknowledged the legitimacy of mighty fifty, from which sprang a line of kin, to wit: forty-nine and forty-eight and forty-seven, forty-six and forty-five, those look-alikes forty-four and forty-three, forty-two and forty-one, and least of that clan, forty, which gave up the ghost to thirty-nine, thirty-eight, thirty-seven, thirty-six, thirty-five, thirty-four, thirty-three, thirty-two, thirty-one and then came thirty, holding position till it could be supplanted by twenty-nine, twenty-eight, twenty-seven, twenty-six, twenty-five, twenty-four, twenty-three, twenty-two, twenty-one and twenty, which was scattered by the energetic teens until at length he had a mere twelve seconds more of his sentence, and then only eleven, which became ten, then short-lived nine and eight and seven and six and five and four, three and two, and now he had but one second to go before he was free!

And the Jailer cheerily said to A. Q. Nameless and to Q. A. Nonamis, as well, "Hey, get your butts outta here!" (But it sounded better in the original Russian.)

LV

THE QUEST FULFiLLED?

With fond farewells to his friend with the Ping Pong ball head, Q. A. Nonamis made his way swift as he could travel to the farm. Both husband and wife gave him hearty greetings and invited him for lunch. At the end of which sumptuous feast, he said he hoped dessert would be Siberian Peach Pie.

"Oh, you haven't heard!" the farmer's wife mourned. "Siberian peach flies attacked every Siberian peach tree. There are no more peaches left to make pies!"

Nonamis was, of course, devastated. He covered his face with his hands and wept bitterly. But after a time he

recalled the wise words John Stone had told his Mama, and, looking up, repeated them, word for word, to the farmer's wife.

But meanwhile, our Nameless hero made his way (gutterwise, Ping Pong ball-headishly) to the spot where he was relieved to perceive that the very same sign was still standing. Namely—

Ye Sign:

SIBERIA RESTAURANT
And yes,
   yet Still **Cooler Inside!**
      But Feel it for Yourself!

Since he had a Nameless hunger, he entered the restaurant and with enormous difficulty (Why do you insist upon details?!) perched himself upon a stool by the counter and squeakified, "Hey, can I, pleaseprettyplease,   place an order?"

At that, the manager made his entrance (Down Center!) but then he regarded the strange Ping Pong ball-headed entity, as did all the other customers in the restaurant, and every one of them screamed and ran out!

LVI

WHY IS THIS CHAPTER DIFFERENT FROM ALL OTHER CHAPTERS?

*O*ur Nameless hero patiently waited upon his stool until the restaurant manager got hold of himself and quakingly reentered.

"Y-y-es?" he quavered.

And A. Q. Nameless at long, long last, shrilled: "Please serve me a slice of Siberian Peach Pie!"

But the manager said, "I'm very sorry, but not only is the Siberian peach crop no more, the only factory in town that used to make it has burned down, and the only baker who knew the recipe died in the fire, so it is absolutely, totally impossible ever again to serve Siberian Peach Pie."

Here, our Nameless hero fell off his stool and pounded his Ping Pong ball head on the floor fifty-four times.[20] But when he stopped, he slithered back to the counter. The manager shook his head and reaffirmed what he said, that there would never ever again be any Siberian Peach Pie, but in a pipsqueaish tone, the Nameless one repeated the words that John Stone told his Mama.

---

[20] One for each chapter up till now

LVii

FiNALE ULTiMO,
i.E.,
YE PUNCHLiNE!

And this is what Q. A. Nonamis and John Stone and our hero, A. Q. Nameless declared—

"Dvoo, gsvm,
R'oo szev
zkkov!" [21]

---

[21] For Cryptic Advice, see Last Words, below

LAST WORDS

PARODIES LAME & BELABOURED

It may well strike the reader that it is wholly egregious in a volume so overstuffed with verbiage to add yet more, but it has been noted[22] that Quest for the Pastried Peach contains many stylistic swipes and lampoons, some of them mere glancing riffs, others enormously belaboured, collectively altogether sophomoric, so for those inclined to care at all about it, below is a guide to these divers parodies.

Proramble— vaguely echoes the opening of Virgil's *The Aeneid*, while foulest strand refers to August Strindberg's *A Dream Play*.

Chapter I— corrupted currents of this world comes from Act III of Shakepeare's *Hamlet*.

Chapter II— syntactical echoes of Ernest Hemingway.

Chapter III— clearly spun off from Charles Lamb's "A Dissertation Upon Roast Pig." Shantih-chant is an oblique echo of T. S. Eliot's poem, "The Waste Land." TastTKossak reflects TastyKakes, a popular dessert in Philadelphia and New Jersey.

Chapter IV— also *Hemingway, specifically, "The Killers."*

Chapter V— parodies the reporting style of Walter Winchell.

---

[22] By Yr. Humble Piescribe.

Chapter VI— spoofs the opening of Herman Melville's *The Encantadas*.

Chapter VII— opening verse echoes Robert Service, but the body of the text is a spinoff on the scholarly fun of *The Pooh Perplex*.

Chapter X— Its purple opening echoes William Peter Blatty's *The Exorcist*.

Chapter XI— see Bram Stoker's "A Hampstead Mystery" passage in *Dracula*.

Chapter XII— patterned on the folk song, "Finnegan's Wake."

Chapter XVIII— first section inspired (?) by the Ferdinand Feghoot tales of "Grendel Briarton," i. e., Reginald Bretnor.

Chapter XXI— see Vachel Lindsay's poem, "The Congo."

Chapter XXIII— referential to this author's books, *The Incredible Umbrella* and *The Amorous Umbrella*.

Chapter XXVIII— Nameless's first lyric is patterned on "Balling the Jack." The Native chorus that follows owes allegiance to an Act II song in Gilbert and Sullivan's *The Gondoliers*.

Chapter XXX – inspired both by Anton Chekhov and Samuel Beckett, specifically, *The Cherry Orchard, The Three Sisters* and *Waiting for Godot*.

Chapter XXII— The title refers to William Beckford's fantasy, Vathek, during which several members of the damned relate their personal histories to one another. Messrs. Dodson and Fogg are presumably descendants of scurrilous attorneys of the same names in Charles Dickens's *The Pickwick Papers*.

Chapter XXIX— The opinion that "seldom" is a discouraging word dates back to when I was a child. I thought the punctuation in the old song, "Home on the Range" must go like this: "Where 'seldom' is heard, a discouraging word."

Chapter XXXIII— The climactic headline is, of course, a belabored pun on lines from Shakespeare's *Julius Caesar*, and while somewhat truncated from the original, is meant to play off, "Cowards die a thousand times; the brave but once."

Chapter XXXIV— This chapter originally was commissioned by the Baltimore Science Fiction Society, Inc., for Balticon 17, the regional science fiction/fantasy convention held annually in or near Baltimore. It appeared on pages 16 and 17 of one of the program booklets.

Chapter XXXV— Special thanks to Toby Sanders, who perpetrated the first draft of this installment, based on an oral devisement by Yr. Humble Piescribe. "The Bridge to the Liver Pies" is one of a series of "Napkin Poems," so called because I wrote most of them when I was an undergraduate student at Penn State, though a few of them came later when I lived in Williamsport, Pennsylvania, and in the first few years in Manhattan. An inexpensive way to entertain a few of my friends, I would ask for a title or an idea and then scrawl a bit of verse on a napkin because we were usually in one of the local diners at the time. Some of the best of the titles were suggested by my late friend Bill Bonham, and this was one of them.

This chapter's climactic pun is, I presume, too obvious to require explication. But just to be sure, here is the original: "Over the river and through the woods, to Grandmama's house we go… "

Chapter XXXVI— In the original correspondence between Yr. Humble Piescribe and Daniel Pinkwater, this was an oral chapter consisting of a recording of an old reel to reel tape that I once had in my collection, but have since lost, though my friend Alan Warren still has a copy. The tape was made at a party, but whether it was in New York or LA, I have no idea. On it, several amusing off-color stories were told by the humorist-actor Henry Morgan, but the highlight was the sharecropper's tale; its narrator was someone named Battle, first name unknown. A search on Yahoo turned up a screenwriter named Norman Battle, so perhaps it was he. At any rate, Battle was (is?) a splendid raconteur. The present chapter is as close to the flavor and language of the original as a notoriously poor memory can devise.

Chapter XXXVII— "Old Hogan's Goat," or substitute "Grogan," I've heard it either way, is an old camping song. The bologna song is traditional, though it took me a long time to track down a version of it that served as the model for the one included in this chapter. Its source: *A Treasury of American Folklore, Vol. XXXIV* and is dated July-September 1921. Its punch-line is quoted by Walt Kelly in *The Pogo Sunday Book.*

Chapter XL— The idea of a Friday night buswash service comes from the early days of my marriage. Saralee and I lived in Williamsport, Pennsylvania, which we found so boring that once as we were passing the local bus station we saw them washing buses, so we stopped and watched, for it was one of the few interesting things we ever witnessed in that town. Many years later in *The Masters of Solitude*, a science fiction epic coauthored with Parke Godwin, I used Williamsport as the model for Lishin, referred to by one character as "a dead vermin-infested city."

The S. T. O. A. are the initials of the Slow Talkers of America, arguably Bob & Ray's funniest comedy routine.

The isle of Usui is named after Mikao Usui, founder of the Japanese system of hands-on healing and energy-channeling known as reiki, of which Yr. Humble Piescribe has attained the rank of mastery. (Cf. www.marvinkaye.com— paid advert.)

Pat's cheesesteaks are one of the best reasons to visit Philadelphia, which, despite the opinion of W. C. Fields, has its, shall we say? distant charms... but then Yr.Humble Piescribe, born there, was lucky enough to move to New York! (Which, to its perhaps single disgrace, has many restaurants that offer thoroughly wretched Philly cheesesteaks y clept. I do know four places in Manhattan that supply the real thing, but that's classified information.)

The footnote's reference to a shaggy dog being like a deep well refers to an old joke in which two monks are seated on either side of the doors of a Buddhist temple, and one says to the other, "Life is like a deep well!" After ten years, the second monk asks, "Why is life like a deep well?" And after another twenty years, the first monk either says (there being two possible punchlines to the story), "All right, have it your way!" or "What? You mean it isn't?"

For details on the non-Euclidian geometrician Nikolai Ivanovich Lobachevsky, either consult wikipedia.com, or, better, the song by Tom Lehrer (who, by the way, in the opinion of Yr. Humble Piescribe, is one of the few humorists who deserve to be mentioned in the verbally accomplished company of W. S. Gilbert, Danny Kaye, Walt Kelly, Daniel Pinkwater, or Peter Schickele.)

"Eigh ba gum" is an expression sometimes employed by Sam Small, a Yorkshire folk hero featured in a series of a delightful fantasy stories collected, though sadly not complete, in *The Flying Yorkshireman*, by (Major) Eric Knight, perhaps best known as the author of Lassie, Come Home. (Now doesn't this dumb book at least provide a liberal education?— Yr. Humble Piescribe)

J. Pierpont Kotzwinkle is an affectionate reference to the writer William Kotzwinkle, but I did not make up the name, Bill did himself. It happened in the late 1950s at Penn State, where Bill was a roommate of my late, lamented friend

Dick Mazza, who got me into theatre in the first place. Bill, one of the shyest, most soft-spoken gentlemen I'd ever met, was one of several volunteer students in an improvisational theatre class that I was also taking. In one of the scenes we did, he loudly declared from offstage, "Make way! I am J. Pierpont Kotzwinkle, and the world is my ash-tray!" For the first time that I had ever witnessed, he totally dominated the scene and all the other actors, myself included. After that, he stayed in that character, which made him ever so much more forceful an individual, and so far as I know, to this very day is still none other than J. Pierpont Kotzwinkle!

"Paragraphs got into all the papers" is a lyric from the Gilbert and Sullivan operetta, *Ruddigore*. It occurs in an Act II duet.

Chapter XLI— The chapter is slightly edited from the original recording to make it read better (a statement which, I am afraid, is altogether hubristic). Not only is it not possible to reproduce the tone of its speaker, except, perhaps, in the reader's imagination, it is also impossible to convey the delivery in which the oral version was stretched out to fill one side of a 30-minute cassette. This was helped along, of course, by the 18-minute silence. If the reason for this gap is no longer understood, the reader may consult "Nixon tapes missing minutes" on yahoo.com.

Chapter XLII— While searching for information about shaggy dog stories on the internet, I went to kith.org, a website that features a section called Shaggy Boxes. This was where I found this variation of the Siberian Peach Pie plot-line; Someone named Ed Bernstein contributed it, and I am grateful to him for sharing this wholly different take on the tale— though the punchline of his version is identical to that known by Yr. Humble Piescribe.

Chapter XLIII— In the original version supplied to me by my former literary agent and esteemed friend William

B. R. Reiss, the protagonist's name was the one I used for his parent. I chose John Stone, instead, partly because I've used so many improbable names in this story I thought one easy name might provide relief. The reason I chose John Stone, is because as I was writing that sequence, I was rehearsing for a Hallowe'en show in which I would pretend to be the British writer E. F. Benson, and read two of his ghost stories, including "The Room in the Tower," which involves a character named Jack Stone.

Chapter XLIV— As the heading suggests, this chapter parodies James Joyce, especially the beginning sequence of *A Portrait of the Artist as a Young Man*.

Chapter XLVI— Most of the "flayfurings" should be easy to figure out, especially if one pronounces them aloud. A few are made up, of course, but a few may be obscure for some readers, therefore let me translate them— Cow daddos = calvados; Golly toby rack u = galatoboureko (one of several possible transliterated spellings), a traditional Greek dessert; Rock-hot la comb = rahat lokum (and spelled other ways, as well), a splendid Turkish confection to which Yr. Humble Piescribe is partial; Tsliver vitch = slivovitz, (the word has a Serbo-Croatian derivation), plum brandy of a high alcoholic content with a literary association— Jonathan Harker drinks it near the beginning of Bram Stoker's *Dracula*.

Chapter XLIX— I have no idea what this chapter's weird style is supposed to represent. Presumably, I did when I sent it to Daniel Pinkwater, but that was a very long time ago.

Chapter L— This chapter, in affectionate memory of one of my all-time favorite authors, William Faulkner, was chiefly suggested by his novel *The Town*, middle volume of the "*Snopes*" trilogy.

The cabin boy who is drowned by his Captain refers to an old folk ballad, "Lowlands."

The reference to pirates being partial to orphans refers, of course, to Gilbert and Sullivan's *The Pirates of Penzance*.

Chapter LI— and once more, Hemingway.

CRYPTIC ADVICE ON THE PUNCHLINE

When I sent the original of this monsterpiece to Daniel Pinkwater, he observed that the punchline was written in an easy to solve substitution code. He then got the last laugh on me because a shaggy jest that does not produce a single groan must be deemed a failure, so he has never reacted to the ending of Siberian Peach Pie in any way whatsoever up to and including this very day!

The punchline is indeed a simple code, which I came upon in my youth when I briefly and reluctantly became a member of the Superman Comics club. (I say reluctantly because I've never quite forgiven them for putting Captain Marvel out of business, he of the Shazam!) The Superman code merely reverses the alphabet, so that A equals Z, B stands for Y, C means X, and so forth. For assistance in translating the punchline of *Quest for the Pastried Peach*, consult the following key—

A BCDEFGHIJKLMNOPQRSTUVWXYZ
ZYXWVUTSRQPONMLKJIHGFEDCBA

A final suggestion— if this ridiculous book drove you crazy, there is a way to get even that might prove satisfactory. Think of someone you know who deserves to suffer, and give it to her, him, or them as a gift. (*paid advert*)

Marvin Kaye
New York City
October 2010

Congratulations!
You survived your

If you enjoyed this book

PLEASE

Post a review on Amazon.
Whether you write a dissertation or just a
few words, you are helping to support this
author's popularity and income.

Please help spread the word.

ABOUT THE AUTHOR

MARVIN KAYE is the author of nineteen novels, including his Dickensian pastiche, *The Last Christmas of Ebenezer Scrooge* and the sequential, *The Passion of Frankenstein,* as well as the terrifying *Fantastique* and *Ghosts of Night and Morning*; the SF cult classics, *The Incredible Umbrella* and (coauthored with Parke Godwin) *The Masters of Solitude,* and the critically-acclaimed mysteries *Bullets for Macbeth* and *My Son the Druggist.* His short story "Ms. Lipshutz and the Goblin," was included in a DAW Books Year's Best Fantasy anthology, and his horrific "The Possession of Immanuel Wolf" was written with the great macabre comedian, Brother Theodore. His numerous best-selling anthologies include *13 Plays of Ghosts and the Supernatural* and other theatre collections; *The Game is Afoot* and other Sherlock Holmes anthologies, and many fantasy/ science fiction books for the Science Fiction Book Club, such as *Ghosts, Masterpieces of Terror and the Supernatural, The Vampire Sextette,* and *The Fair Folk,* which won the World Fantasy Award for Best Anthology of 2006. His column,

"Marvin Kaye's Nth Dimension," appears online at *http://spaceandtimemagazine.com.*

Thanks to permission from The Rex Stout Estate, he has written more than twenty new Nero Wolfe mystery stories and is working on more. He is the editor of *Sherlock Holmes Mystery Magazine,* and both editor and copublisher of America's oldest supernatural periodical, *Weird Tales* magazine (dating back to 1923!)

A native of Philadelphia, PA., he is a graduate of Penn State, with an M. A. in theatre and English literature; he formerly headed the tutoring staff of the Manhattan campus of Mercy College; taught magic and mindreading showmanship at The New School; for twenty-three years was Adjunct Professor of Creative Writing at New York University, has taught mystery writing in England for the Smithsonian Institute, has served as a judge for the Edgar, International Thriller Writers, Nero and World Fantasy Awards and is Artistic Director for The Open Book, New York's oldest readers theatre company.

As an actor/director, he is Creative Director of The Open Book, New York's oldest readers theatre ensemble, now in its 48th year. In addition to acting in its productions, he has appeared on Broadway with Dame Edna; off-Broadway as a producer of three critically-acclaimed shows, and as a magician did shows in area hospitals and old age homes, as well as three seasons as a solo magic performer at the Sharon Playhouse in Sharon, Connecticut. His television credits include "The Cowboy's West" with Max Morath and as a mental magic performer on talk shows in Boston and New York City.

He is listed in *Who's Who in America, Who's Who in Entertainment, Who's Who in the East, Who's Who in Business and Industry,* et cetera – and most recently the *Who's Who Lifetime Achievement* listing.

ALSO BY MARVIN KAYE

The Hillary Quayle Mysteries:
A Lively Game of Death
The Grand Ole Opry Murders
Bullets for Macbeth
The Laurel & Hardy Murders
The Soap Opera Slaughters

The Marty Gold Mysteries:
My Son The Druggist
My Brother The Druggist

The Masters of Solitude trilogy:
The Masters of Solitude (with Parke Godwin)
Wintermind, 1982 (with Parke Godwin)
Singer Among the Nightingales (with Parke Godwin)

The Incredible Umbrella series:
The Incredible Umbrella
The Amorous Umbrella
The Incredible Umbrella Tetralogy

Other novels:
A Cold Blue Light (with Parke Godwin)
Ghosts Of Night And Morning
Fantastique
The Last Christmas Of Ebenezer Scrooge
Quest For The Pastried Peach

Edited Anthologies, short fiction and non-fiction titles too numerous to list.

iF YOU LOVED THE BOOK

YOU'LL REALLY LOVE THE AUDiOBOOK!

Unabridged, with Sound Effects and Music

Performed by

Jon Koons

Available from audible.com

Winter 2020/21

Metamorphic Press

We Only Print
Good Stuff!

*Irreverent Humor
(first time
in print
since 1976)*

*Irrelevent Humor
from award
winning author
Marvin Kaye*

*Humorous
SciFi
YA*

*Historical
Fiction*

Classics

*Stories for
Adults*

*Stories for
Kids*

*Inspirational
Pads and
Journals*

More to come!
metamorphicpress.com

www.ingramcontent.com/pod-product-compliance
Lightning Source LLC
Chambersburg PA
CBHW020256130626
46549CB00005B/2232